Praise for the Guardian of the Gods duology

"A lost priestess, magic storytellers, godkillers, and a
secret that could upend the world. Tobi Ogundiran
has woven together a masterful fantasy epic of lost
faith, found family, and a cosmic war—with hints of
more to come. This is one to add to your reading list!"

P. Djèlí Clark, award-winning author of *A Master of Djinn*

"The most spectacular part of the book is. . .Ashâke
herself: her anger at the silent gods, her slow journey to
find out who she is without the temple, and finally her
discovery of her own true power."

The Washington Post

"Immersive, entertaining, and well-crafted, with an
atmospheric tone and an intriguing cast of characters, *In the
Shadow of the Fall* is a small African epic fantasy with big
scope and big stakes, and I look forward to its conclusion."

Wole Talabi for *Locus*

"The novella of the year has arrived! Ogundiran's story of an acolyte's lost faith is electrifying, terrifying, and tender all at the same time. There's more wonder and creativity packed into these pages than a book five times its length, and I'm already aching for the next chapter in Ashâke's adventure."

Mark Oshiro, award-winning author of
Anger Is a Gift and *Each of Us a Desert*

"Ogundiran unveils a world that is both in recovery and on the cusp of collapse, a brilliant tension that he reinforces with a propulsive plot, dynamic imagery, and a protagonist who holds within her the seeds of hope. I'm already looking forward to book two."

Moses Ose Utomi, author of *Daughters of Oduma*
and *The Lies of the Ajungo*

"A sure hit for fans of Suyi Davies Okungbowa, Moses Ose Utomi, and N.K. Jemisin."

Booklist

AT THE FOUNT
OF CREATION

Also by Tobi Ogundiran
and available from Titan Books:

IN THE SHADOW OF THE FALL

AT THE
FOUNT OF
CREATION

TOBI OGUNDIRAN

TITAN BOOKS

At the Fount of Creation
Print edition ISBN: 9781835411070
E-book edition ISBN: 9781835413142

Published by Titan Books
A division of Titan Publishing Group Ltd
144 Southwark Street, London SE1 0UP
www.titanbooks.com

First Titan edition: January 2025
10 9 8 7 6 5 4 3 2 1

A CIP catalogue record for this title is available from the British Library.

Printed and bound by CPI Group (UK) Ltd, Croydon, CR0 4YY.

For Keosha

As flies to wanton boys are we to th' gods;
They kill us for their sport.

—William Shakespeare,
King Lear

All gods dispense suffering without reason.
Otherwise they would not be worshipped.
Through indiscriminate suffering men know
fear and fear is the most divine emotion. It is the
stones for altars and the beginning of wisdom . . .
Real gods require blood.

—Zora Neale Hurston,
Their Eyes Were Watching God

Four Hundred Seasons Ago

First came a terrible sound. The shriek of thunder, of fury, that rocked the world. Then came red lightning; night turned to day as a thousand bolts fractured the heavens and rained down on Aye. In the grand city of Ile-Ife, which is the first city, they cleaved the Tower, crushing thousands to death. And where they touched ground across the vast continent, the villages and cities and abodes of men went up in great flames.

Yet more lightning forked into the Endless Sea, travelling down, down, past schools of fish and herds of nameless beasts, past old swollen bones and ruins of long sunk ships. It went into the fathomless deep, until it touched the very roots of the world, which took its energy, which was the pure and righteous fury of terrible Shango.

The world broke.

The sea erupted and the continent succumbed to it. The sea churned and boiled and opened channels that became gullies that broke the continent into islands. And that which was in the sea was exposed to air.

At the bottommost part of the sea where old things lay was a rock the size of three elephants. Shaken from where it had lodged, it rolled and tumbled, buoyed by restless waves, by a sea come alive. Up and up it was raised, over the mountains that lurked in the deep, until it broke the surface and beached ashore beneath the barren limbs of an elder tree.

And there it glowed, beautiful, terrible; as white as the sun.

A crack appeared in the centre of the boulder. A hair's breadth, such that only a keen eye might see it. Soon it widened, running in a seam down the length of the boulder. Bits of glowing rock broke off to hiss and smoke against the black beach. A hand emerged. It wiggled, a serpent's tongue tasting air, then gripped the edge of the rock. Out came another hand that began to push, widening the crack until like a fruit, like a pod, with an almighty crack, the rock broke cleanly in two.

Out squirmed a figure. He was a hideous thing, neither man nor beast; he was gaunt, with ribs that strained against a paper-thin skin as he crawled from his prison. Farther and farther he dragged himself, his body cutting a track in the black beach. He raised his face to the sky. Where both eyes should be were ruined orifices, puckered and unseeing; where his mouth should be was a ruinous gash, sewn shut with copper threads.

This was his first face.

At the back of his head was a second face, whose eyes were black voids save for the fiery irises that burned like rings of fire in a starless night; whose lips were full of guile and cunning.

The orisha crawled through the black sand away from his rocky prison, away from the tree and down the meadow. He reached the dirt road and collapsed.

And here he remained for a few moments that might have been an eternity.

The Town Crier

Garuba flicked his tongue, probing the inside of his waterskin. He sucked desperately, but it was empty. The old leather was as parched as the desert around him. A strangled sound escaped his lips, something between a cry and a moan. Never had he been so thirsty in all his life, and that was saying something, coming from a kingdom where water was severely rationed. It didn't help that the sun beat down relentlessly. He began to lick his skin. It was incredibly salty, and did nothing to quench his thirst, but he needed water and his sweat was the only liquid around.

Garuba couldn't say exactly when he had lost his way. He had left Oyo with the other town criers, following the Oba's Road before they were dispatched in various directions to other villages scattered across the kingdom. As a crier he had walked all over the kingdom; he knew the routes like the back of his hand, and could have found his way to any village even with his eyes closed. Which made it strange that he found himself lost in the desert, nothing but cracked, barren earth stretching as far as his eye could see. It seemed the world was just this desert, and he was the last man in it.

The sun bore down relentlessly, burning his skin, baking the earth so hard that the very air shimmered. Something appeared in the distance, silvery-white under the sunlight. A pool. Garuba blinked the sweat from his eyes. He closed his eyes, opened them. The pool still lay there, beckoning to him. But it wasn't real. He knew better now. Oases and lakes did not exist where rain did not fall, not on this island, not in this kingdom. Garuba didn't know if he was going mad from the heat, or from thirst, or from hunger. But he was going mad.

He stumbled and fell. His satchel flew from his shoulders, and out came his gong, two pieces of bitter kola, a fresh tunic and the embroidered kerchief that his daughter had made for him, and his empty waterskin. He lay there, cheek pressed against the cracked earth. He would not rise again. He had neither the will nor the strength.

"Rain," he mumbled. "Rain . . ."

Ilorin hadn't seen rainfall in seasons. To Garuba, rain was an alien phenomenon, as alien as the liquid fire that was said to have sputtered from mountains seasons ago. He couldn't fathom water falling from the skies. Fresh water existed only in melo-pods, those hardy fruits that dug deep into the earth and extracted water.

But it hadn't always been so. Countless seasons ago, as the elders said, they would pray and sacrifice to Oya, and she would conjure up strong westerly winds that blew rain clouds from the Endless Sea over the land. And it would rain, and crops would flourish, and fruits would grow. But most importantly, there would be an abundance of fresh water. Their lakes and streams and rivers would overflow. But here in Ilorin they had forgotten the gods. Well . . . not so much forgotten as *believed* them dead. And they had suffered for it.

He still remembered the sight of those boats sailing towards them. The alarm had sounded, and the small folk had clustered ashore, watching with apprehension as a small woman with kind eyes stepped off a boat and announced that they were griots, come to deliver good news. Ilorin was a small island so removed from the other kingdoms as to be isolated. They hadn't seen an outsider in seasons, much less griots, who they believed had gone the way of the gods: a thing of an age past.

But here were real griots, insisting that the gods still lived. Garuba had heard the Song, seen firsthand the Memory of that girl covered in glyphs, of the orisha appearing next to her. But most importantly, he had seen her call the wind, and he had been caught in powerful rapture.

Oba Adeyanju had dispatched the criers immediately, to go to every corner of the kingdom ahead of the griots to deliver the news. The gods were alive. They lived in the

Guardian. And Garuba had been only too happy to go, to be the bearer of good news. As his baba had been, and his baba's baba before him.

"Oya," Garuba whispered, licking the crust from his lips. "Orisha iya mi. I ask for rain. Please."

I am going to die, he thought.

His mind went to Tutu, his daughter. He began to weep; dry, weak heavings. Who would provide for her in his absence? Who would—?

A shadow fell over him.

Garuba mustered the last of his strength and flipped over. A man was standing over him; Garuba could not make out his features. As the darkness claimed him, Garuba told himself that like the disappearing pools, this, too, was a hallucination.

I'm dead, thought Garuba as he came to. Everywhere was dark. But then he made out the stars, twinkling in an ink-black sky, made out a jaundiced moon, and realised that he was not dead.

He was still in the desert. He sat up, nearly blacked out from the sudden movement. That was when he saw the stone basin, brimming with water. Garuba moved without thought, scrambling off the bench and towards the basin. He dipped a hand into it. The water was cool against his skin. It was real. Real.

And then he was drinking, scooping up handful after handful as he gulped. *Great undead gods!* Never had water tasted so sweet! He began to weep, slobbering as he drank, blessing the name of every orisha he could think of for sparing him. Garuba cupped his hands and spooned water to his lips. And, when that was not enough, dunked his head into the basin and lapped like an animal until his belly filled to where it hurt. Only then did he collapse against the stone bench, panting and slightly delirious.

That was when he saw the man.

"Ah," said the stranger, grinning at Garuba. "Thirsty, are we?"

The stranger wore a flowing black kaftan, a red scarf wrapped around his throat. Seven heavy golden locs framed a face of indeterminate age. Sometimes when the fire moved just right he looked like a young man, and other times he looked old. An old scar ran down his face.

"Forgive me," Garuba croaked at last.

"Nothing to forgive," said the stranger amiably. "I know only too well what it means to thirst." He reached behind him and produced a tray bursting with fruits. "Fruit?"

Garuba, tentative, picked an apple.

"I am Garuba Oyeyemi. Chief town crier of Ilorin. I set out from Ilorin"—what was it now, three, four days ago? He couldn't tell. His memory was all a blur—"some days ago. At the behest of the Oba. He told us to deliver the griots' message: the gods are alive."

The stranger seemed unfazed by the news. He seemed instead like he had heard Garuba remark that the sky was blue. This was not the reaction Garuba had expected.

"Did you . . . did you already hear this?" asked Garuba. "The gods still live. I saw with mine own eyes! The griots—"

"Yes, yes. I heard you." The man's face shifted, and Garuba thought he saw a flash of anger. But it was gone just as quickly, and he was offering Garuba another fruit.

"Apologies, my friend. I did not catch your name."

"What is the point of a god?"

Garuba blinked, wondering what manner of question that was. "The point of a god? To . . . to provide," he said with religious fervour. "What else? We owe them our lives. We owe them . . . everything."

"But don't you want a world where you are not beholden to the whims of a god? Don't you want a better life for Tutu?"

The apple soured in Garuba's mouth. "How do you . . . how do you know of my daughter? How do you know her *name*?"

"I know a great many things," said the stranger.

"Who . . . are you?"

The stranger's smile was terrible. "I think, Garuba, you know who I am."

Garuba swallowed, asked in a quiet voice, "Are you . . . a god?"

The stranger looked irritated. "I am more than a god.

The orisha are the moon. And I am the sun, enduring, everlasting."

A cold current travelled down Garuba's spine. *Godkiller.* Here was a godkiller before him, but Garuba could not bring himself to say the word.

"I have many names," the stranger continued. "My parents named me Yinka, and I bore this name when I lived as a man. When I was born anew, I took the name Bahl'ul for myself." He prodded the fire, flames dancing in his eyes. "My followers call me Teacher."

"You!" Garuba scrambled backwards, the word bursting at last from his mouth. "Godkiller!"

"What is interesting," the stranger continued, "is I have only ever killed one of the orisha. The Supreme Father himself. The others . . . well, they fell to the blades of my followers."

Garuba was caught in a nightmare. Why did he have to meet this man? What manner of man would talk so casually about murdering the Supreme Father? But then . . . he said it himself. He was not a man. He was not even a god.

"You . . . you confused the road." Of course, it made all the sense in the world now. These were roads he had travelled countless times, roads he knew like the back of his hand. And yet he had gotten lost. But he hadn't, he really hadn't. Garuba looked into the Teacher's eyes and a fresh wave of terror poured over him. How did he manage such a thing? What kind of power did he possess?

The Teacher smiled and Garuba would have sworn on his baba's dead bones that he had read his mind.

"What . . ." Garuba licked his crusted lips. "What do you want with me?"

"To do what you do best, Garuba," said the Teacher softly. "Deliver a message." He pondered for a moment. "Do you know what I cherish most about mortals? Rationality. Gods, not so much. They do not think as mortals do, nor do they abide by our rules. But you, Garuba, are a rational man, yes?"

"Yes," he croaked.

"Excellent. I am really glad that we understand each other. You will continue on to Akure. But when you arrive, you will not tell them that the gods still live. You will not sing of hope or any such nonsense. You must deliver instead the following news . . ."

He leaned in, and whispered in Garuba's ear.

"But what of the griots?" Garuba asked, once the Teacher was done. "We are only the vanguard. They'll show the Memory; the people will see for themselves."

The Teacher rose to his feet.

"Do as I've told you, and leave the griots to me."

ONE

The city, Ile-Ife, lay in ruins.

But that was to be expected, reasoned Ashâke, of a place that had suffered the brunt of Shango's wrath. Half the city lay buried beneath rubble, and what must once have been formidable edifices were now small mountains of charred debris, barely distinguishable from the destruction that surrounded them. Still other structures remained oddly preserved: cracked, desiccated fountains that had not seen water for four hundred seasons; establishments that had once been the haunts of the citizens of Ile-Ife; here and there the odd bathhouse. And of course, the Tower—or what was left of it.

The Tower of the Orisha was a slender edifice of black granite that swelled from the city centre, its sleek length truncated to the tips of jagged edges that pierced the night sky. From this angle it seemed the moon balanced in a precarious perch right on the Tower, such that the slightest movement would send the globe toppling over onto the world below.

"Well," said Arewa, lord of beauty and debauchery, a little too loudly. "Shouldn't have built the blasted Tower, I'll tell you that. But Father . . . he wanted to—what were his words?—'enjoy direct communion with man.'" He hiccupped, then raised his gourd in the general direction of the Tower. "Here's to communion." And he burst into tinkling titters that carried across the silent streets.

"Shut up," growled Ogun, lord of war and metalworking.

"Don't tell me to shut up. I'm not some mortal—"

Ogun shot him a look and he fell silent. "Don't think I'm scared of you," he muttered, then, catching Ashâke's eye, winked. He brought his gourd to his lips and took a messy swig, white foam dribbling into his beard.

Arewa was beautiful. Painfully beautiful. And he knew it. His rich ebon skin was unblemished and his lips were full and his kohled eyes were dark pools that seemed to suck in whoever was looking. Once or twice Ashâke had found herself gazing longingly into those eyes only to realise, slightly flustered, that he had been doing it on purpose! But Arewa was also the lord of wine and drunks, and as such always seemed just on the cusp of inebriation. It did not help that he drank constantly from a gourd—one that never seemed to empty.

Though Ashâke had now spent six moons with the orisha, constantly in their presence, hearing their voices in her head—or, when they manifested, interacting physically with them—she still found herself in awe of them. Ogun was near seven feet tall and always manifested wearing nothing but a loincloth, clutching a war hammer that was as long as Ashâke was tall, and looked twice as heavy. The prickly lord of war and metalworking, when not brooding, glared openly at everything and at nothing. He had been close to Shango and both had shared a quick temper. Ashâke knew Ogun was just spoiling to have his chance at revenge. Oya, goddess of winds and rain, was a vision of serenity, a beautiful collar about her neck. Once, when Ashâke had inquired about it, she had replied vaguely that a lover had gifted it to her. And then there was Yemoja. Calculating, vengeful Yemoja, whose shrewd leadership and singular vision of retribution had sent them across seven kingdoms in six moons.

The orisha were in Ashâke. In a way, they *were* her, as she was them. She felt each and every one of their emotions, could channel their powers. They were interwoven in every way that mattered. Thankfully, they could not read her mind. Ashâke was not sure she would enjoy having them privy to her thoughts. The others still slumbered; she felt their weak essence as they clung on to life. But these four were still strong enough to manifest physically, and it was these four who had been her companions these past six moons.

Six moons of travelling Aye, of questing after elusive answers. First they had gone to Ijesha, a small island kingdom off the coast of Akure. Then they had gone to Tesse. At each turn they came up with more questions than answers. Who were the followers? How did they grow so powerful? What were the limits to their powers? How could they be destroyed? The lack of answers was frustrating. Ashâke felt and saw the orisha's frustration grow each day. Her own frustrations only grew at the endless quest, sleeping in hard barns and on the rocky earth beneath open sky, constantly on the lookout for godkillers. No one knew who the godkillers were, nor did they know the man they followed, the one who called himself the Teacher. It was as though they had simply come into existence from nowhere.

Or they had always existed.

Dark structures loomed out of the night as they made their way towards the Tower. And here, closer to the heart of the city, a strange growth had taken hold. Woody and invasive, the growth climbed and curled over buildings, ripped through the streets, knitting and crisscrossing so it looked like the great web of some gargantuan spider, or the desiccated remains of some long-forgotten beast of yore.

"What is this?" asked Ashâke, picking her way down the street, stepping through the growth.

"Trees," said Oya. "Dead trees."

Their footfalls echoed on the broken street. Perhaps it was the strange quiet of the streets, or the strange emptiness of the houses, or the strange riblike growth, but Ashâke felt her eyes constantly wandering to the shadows that repelled moonlight, to the dark jagged windows that looked out like hollow eyes. A sense of uneasiness came over her, and after a moment or two she realised what it was.

"There are no animals," Ashâke whispered. "We're far into the city and I haven't seen a single animal."

"Smart creatures," said Arewa. "Nothing good to be found here. Only reminders of our broken past. An absence of life. The sooner we abandon this graveyard—"

A woman stood in the middle of the street. She hadn't been there a moment ago, Ashâke was sure of it. Yet here she was, a woman of about sixty seasons, leaf-green iro and buba draped across her tall, lean form. Several loops of coral beads adorned her neck and wrists, and a white circle had been drawn around her left eye. She gazed unflinchingly at Ashâke.

"Welcome, Guardian."

Her voice rang loud. Too loud in the quiet street.

Cold hands clawed down Ashâke's spine. She glanced at the orisha but they had vanished, relinquishing their physical manifestations. As they did not know who the godkillers were, the orisha had decided early on to err on the side of discretion, never manifesting in the presence of others, having Ashâke dress to cover her etchings so that anyone who looked upon her would not see her for what she was. The Guardian. Which made it all the more unnerving that this stranger saw through her.

Do not speak, Yemoja hissed. *Do not confirm that you're the Guardian. They could be hunting us.*

And there could be others lurking in the shadows, offered Arewa wisely.

Ashâke cast wildly around, panic stealing into her heart. She still suffered nightmares of the massacre on the riverbank, of the frozen, calcified griots, of Baale Jaha's face curdling as he took in the etchings on her skin, as he realised that she was the reason for the massacre. She had spent moons dreading her next encounter with godkillers knowing she was not ready to face them.

"Something is not right . . ." she muttered. The woman stood a little too still, her back too straight, her gaze unblinking. And then Ashâke started towards the woman.

Alarm spiked through Ashâke as she approached; the orisha's emotions overwhelming her even as they screamed at her.

What are you doing? Have you lost your mind?

But Ashâke was already in front of the woman. Up close she could see the tribal scarifications on her face, the gold ring that pierced her nose, the dark eyes full of sadness. They were so close now that Ashâke should feel the heat rising off her skin. But she felt nothing. She reached out a tremulous hand . . . and it passed right through the woman.

"She's not real," Ashâke whispered. Relief flooded her

body, and it was only then she realised she had been tense, her muscles coiled for flight.

"A farahàn," said Oya, who had manifested and was walking around the woman, inspecting her like some odd bird in a menagerie. "Old magic. I haven't seen the like in . . . well, in a long time. This was how the griots of old left messages for themselves."

"So . . . she's a griot?" asked Ashâke.

"It would seem so. But griots don't often leave impressions of themselves."

"Why?"

"Because they die shortly after," said Yemoja. She glanced slantwise at Ashâke. "Think of farahàns as spectres, tied to a place. They cannot leave until they have delivered their message."

Ashâke looked back at the woman, even as she felt the gods quicken with excitement. Finally some answers. But what message could have been so important that she gave her life?

"Who are you?" asked Yemoja. "Speak, farahàn. I command you."

The woman looked at Yemoja, then back at Ashâke. "I think . . . I think she'll only respond to me," said Ashâke.

Yemoja glowered. "And why is that?"

"Maybe because she addressed her?" said Arewa. "Called her Guardian?"

Yemoja's eyes were chips of ice, and Ashâke felt her

annoyance, a sour taste at the back of her throat. She did not like to be disobeyed and Ashâke had disobeyed, endangered them all by approaching the farahàn. She was not likely to forget that soon. She waved her hand. "Go ahead, then."

Ashâke bowed her head in deference, then turned back to the farahàn. "Who are you?"

"I am Oluremi Adebisi," said the woman. "Master Griot of Jebba clan. I have waited a long time for you, Guardian."

How long was a long time? As if reading her thoughts, the farahàn responded. "Three moons have passed since the Fall. Four since I took this message."

"Stars above," breathed Ashâke. "So you've been here for four hundred seasons just . . . waiting for me?"

"Three moons have passed since the Fall. Four since I took this message."

"Ask what the message is," said Yemoja.

Ashâke started to ask, then paused, frowning. "Only my mother knew I was—*am*—the Guardian. And she kept that secret close, even from other priests. Griots certainly did not know that a Guardian existed, much less know that it was me."

"Certainly not three moons after the Fall," growled Ogun.

"Precisely." She turned to the farahàn. "How do you know who I am? And . . . why have you been waiting for me?"

The woman took a step forwards, then walked right through Ashâke and down the street. They scurried after her.

"After the Fall," said the woman, "we remained here in Ile-Ife, picking through the rubble for survivors. In the ruins of the city we found some of our people who had attended the Conclave. Many of them perished, but not before they told us of the attack so we could make a Memory. Some of us tried to leave this place, but the sea still boiled and the skies still wept blood and Shango's Flames still burned. So we remained here for moons and moons. We thought we were the last people alive . . . until he came."

"The Teacher?" asked Ashâke.

"An orisha."

A moment's shocked silence followed as they digested the farahàn's words.

"Impossible," said Yemoja. "I rounded up every one of us."

"Apparently not," muttered Arewa into his gourd.

"Shut up," she snapped. "You forget the reason I created *her*"—she jabbed in Ashâke's direction—"was because Olodumare was dead. We needed a way to walk Aye, to exist without—without losing ourselves!"

"Then perhaps this orisha, whoever he is, has an idan," Ogun suggested. "His own Guardian?"

Yemoja snorted in derision. As Ashâke had come to learn, the creation of an idan—a living, breathing idan such as her—was not so easy. With Olodumare and Shango dead Yemoja was the most powerful of the existing orisha, and it had taken everything to create Ashâke, weakened her so greatly that Iyalawo had been able to overpower her and lock them away.

"He didn't have an idan," said Ashâke. "The orisha, he walks without an idan."

They considered the implication.

"Who?" said Yemoja. "Ask her the name of this orisha."

The woman cocked her head, eyelids fluttering like bird wings. "An orisha."

"Yes but *who*? Which one?" Yemoja's hair had ballooned out from her head. Ashâke repeated the question and once again the farahàn cocked her head, blinked rapidly a few times, and said, "An orisha."

Yemoja cursed.

"Easy, Mother," said Oya. "I don't know of farahàns staying this long. It is probably decaying."

They were now walking at a decline through what used to be the residential area, past crumbling houses. The broken remains of the Tower loomed ever in sight.

"Where is she taking us?"

"To our grisly end," said Arewa, meeting their glares with a beautiful smile.

The farahàn led them into a small house, past a small room filled with broken furniture and a massive water pot, and into an even smaller room. As they squeezed into the low room Ashâke's eyes adjusted to the dark and she saw, on a rotted bed, the remains of a body.

"It is her," said Ashâke. "The farahàn."

The woman's clothes were now faded into a dull grey, the pattern barely discernible in the low light. Ashâke recognised her only by the loops of coral beads and nose ring.

"What is that?" asked Ogun.

In the skeleton's hands was something. Ashâke reached out and took it, holding it up to the light. "A rock?"

It wasn't quite a rock. As large as a chicken's egg, it looked at once transparent, like frozen water, and like silver.

The farahàn's mouth moved but words only came out sporadically, so that they could scarcely make sense of what she was saying. ". . . give . . . and take this . . . to find . . ."

"What?" cried Yemoja. "Find what?"

". . . give . . . and take this . . . to find . . ."

The farahàn cast around one last time, and a look of peace came on her face. Then she dispersed, dissolving into smoke.

TWO

Half a moon after leaving Ile-Ife, they remained at a loss as to the nature or purpose of the object.

"It is not metal," said Ogun, turning the transparent, strangely silvery piece in his hands. "At least not any kind that I know of."

"Perhaps it is a . . . compass of sorts?" suggested Oya. "To help us find this orisha, whoever he is."

There was also the matter of an orisha roaming free.

"If he hasn't fallen to the godkillers," said Yemoja. "I refuse to believe this orisha managed to survive on his own when . . ."

When they couldn't. Yemoja was nothing if not proud, and Ashâke saw every day how their situation wounded her. Mighty gods reduced to running, depending on *her*, a mortal, for their survival. But there was no denying the rock.

They kept moving, never remaining in one place too long. One evening Ashâke saw Inysha in the distance, the mighty city clustered on the lips of the Endless Sea, and her heart yearned for Simbi. Six moons ago Ashâke had been there, but the orisha had been newly awakened, and she had just arrived with the survivors of the massacre and there had been so much on her mind that she had forgotten about Simbi. But now . . . they were *so close*. She did not know when next she might get such an opportunity. And she was tired of running in circles.

"We should go to Inysha."

"Why?" asked Oya. She was lounging in the tall grass, several butterflies fluttering around her. She made a sport of catching and releasing them, her face awash with a child's wonder and delight.

Ashâke licked her lips. The gods were not privy to her thoughts but they could tell when she was lying. "We may find answers there."

"And we may find answers if we peered hard enough at the moon," Yemoja remarked. Arewa snorted into his gourd.

"Ireti, Mama Agba's sister—she's a griot, and there are other griots in the city. She—they may . . . know something about this object."

Yemoja was squinting suspiciously at her.

"I am here to serve," Ashâke said quickly. "It may well be that there's nothing there. But if there is, and we missed it because—" *Because you are too hardheaded.*

"She's right," said Ogun. He was leaning on his hammer and scowling into the distance.

And so it was settled. At the first crow of the cock they made their way towards Inysha to find Ireti. A giddy excitement overcame Ashâke the closer they drew to the city and she tried hard not to show it. She couldn't let the gods know her real reason for wanting to visit Inysha. The prospect of seeing Ireti, of seeing Ralia . . . she would love to see how the children were faring; if, like her, they suffered nightmares. Though Ashâke could not imagine how one could witness such things and remain unscathed.

It was near noon when they entered Inysha and it didn't take long for Ashâke to notice a change in the air. When last she had been here the streets had been alive with the tinkling laughter of playing children, the many-dialected cries of traders plying their wares, of friends and acquaintances calling out to each other, all commingling to provide the general air of a prosperous, if raucous, city. Now, though . . . all these still existed, but marred with a palpable undercurrent of malice, of fear. Fewer children roamed the streets, and what tradesmen remained peered out from their stalls with suspicion.

Something is not right, said Oya.

Ashâke pulled her scarf tighter and hurried into the next street.

Declarations like SEVEN CURSES UPON THE GODS and DEATH TO BELIEVERS had been daubed over shops and taverns and other establishments, always in red paint, which Ashâke had first feared was blood. Just up ahead a young boy of no more than seven seasons was seated atop his baba's shoulders as he smeared curses and blasphemous pronouncements over the lintel of their home.

It was madness.

Ashâke kept her head down, her scarf low as she kept to the shadows and tried as much as possible to draw no attention to herself. This was not the Inysha she had come to nearly six moons ago, two dozen orphans in trail, banging at Ireti's door. This was not the Inysha she had dreamed of settling in with Simbi. It was . . . wrong. The very air seemed alive with malice.

This is the work of godkillers, growled Ogun. *They have turned the people against us.*

We must leave, said Yemoja. *Now.*

"But Ireti—"

We can trust no one.

As Ashâke came round the bend her heart stopped cold. Nailed to a post was a charcoal drawing of her. She stood in a boat, her lifted arms vanishing into a cloud of dark scribbles, which she knew represented the wind. The wind she had summoned to buoy them to safety. And just beneath the crude rendering, scrawled in a vicious hand were the words:

DEATH TO THE GUARDIAN

Ashâke felt queasy. Her knees grew weak and it seemed as though the world were spinning. The sun was suddenly too bright, the voices too loud. She didn't understand. Why did they want her dead? But the answer to that question was all too obvious: she carried the orisha within her. But why did the people want them dead? This was not the reaction she had expected. She had expected the people to rejoice as she had to learn that the gods still lived, that there was yet hope. Instead, it seemed that they had turned against them. Turned against *her*. And . . . how did they know what she looked like?

But of course the griots had Sang their Song, shown the Memory. That meant everyone knew what she looked like.

Including the godkillers.

Ashâke felt suddenly exposed. She cast about her, expecting godkillers to slink out of the alcoves and stalls, angling straight for her. She jumped at a sudden bark of laughter, but it was only a drunk and his friend, jesting as they staggered arm in arm down the street.

Gods, thought Ashâke. *Good merciful gods.*

She stumbled away, breathing hard, struggling to keep both feet beneath her. *Walk,* she told herself. *Just keep walking and act normal.* But how could she act normal when her breath came in short, strained gasps? How could she act normal when it felt like a fist had closed around her throat, like an elephant was crushing her chest? She reached up, seeking her scarf, wanting to throw it off, *rip* it off, wanting for one gulp of fresh air to help clear her vision—

"Young woman," a concerned voice said. "Are you okay?"

"Yes," Ashâke gasped, throwing off the hand before it gained purchase. "Yes . . . I'm—"

She fled into the next street.

And suddenly she was surrounded, hemmed in by a sea of people. Around her was a swarm, a great horde, and they were moving in the opposite direction. Alarmed, she tried to push through, but the throng moved as if of a single mind, and then her feet were not on the ground, so that she was swept farther from the gates.

"Where—where are we going?"

"Didn't you hear?" Someone's fishy breath in her face; a spray of spit. "The Ogboni caught some priests!"

"What—?"

Ashâke had no idea who the Ogboni were. But they had caught priests, and she thought she had an idea what was coming.

She would use her powers. For some strange reason whenever she invoked her powers, though, the followers were not usually far behind. It had led them to her where they had slain the griots on the riverbank, and it had led them to her in Ijesha where she'd escaped by the skin of her teeth. The last thing she needed right now was to have godkillers—however many they numbered in Inysha—swarming towards her.

The crowd poured into the square. A vast circular space, flanked on the left by the stone facade of the House of Chiefs, and on the right by what used to be a temple, its sleek exterior defaced by paintings of a strange and vicious jackal head. Often used for festivities, or when the oba wanted to address his subjects, now the square teemed with Inyshini: men and women and children, old and young, all of them caught in the throes of a frightening, rabid fervour. In the distance Ashâke could just make out the palace, polished limestone walls gleaming in the sun.

A platform had been erected in the centre of the square, and three shackled priests were kneeling on it. Ashâke knew them by their white raiments, now bloodied and torn. An elderly priest knelt at the far end, his scalp shining a bright crimson, as though someone had dragged him so viciously by the hair that it tore from the roots. Next to him knelt a woman, and she stared so resolutely at the ground that she might as well have been in communion with the gods. The third was a boy so young that were he not garbed in priestly white, Ashâke might have taken him for an acolyte. He looked around, eyes wide with fear, tears leaking down oily cheeks. His eyes danced wildly over the crowd, as though seeking mercy, compassion. But there was no mercy to be found here, not from this pack of bloodthirsty jackals.

Several guards surrounded the platform, clutching long spears and bronze shields. Ashâke wondered if they were there to keep the crowd back or to stop the priests from escaping. But it did not matter. Their very presence confirmed what she had feared: the oba was complicit in this persecution.

A town crier clambered onto the platform and struck his gong: a harsh clang rent the noon air, and in the wake of its resonance came a terrible hush. He withdrew.

Someone stepped onto the platform, brushing past the kneeling priests until he stood before the gathered crowd. And though he no longer wore a watchman's light buba and shokoto but a rich kaftan of Kongi blue, and though he no longer wore his hair in a plait but let it hang loose around his shoulders, his face was one Ashâke would recognise anywhere.

Djola.

Ashâke gasped. For a moment her heart gave a lurch of joy at the sight of that familiar face. But the moment passed, as reason came back to her. Djola was dead, his body stolen by Yaruddin, that fucking parasite, who was now desecrating his memory.

A hot tongue of rage flared up Ashâke's throat and she forgot her fear, forgot that she was surrounded by enemies. What she wouldn't give to kill that bastard, that body-snatching leech. What she wouldn't give to inflict such unimaginable pain on him that he begged for the release of death. She wished for Shango's lightning, for his all-consuming flames.

"My brothers! My sisters!" Djola's voice rang clear over the square. Overhead, vultures cried as they circled the platform. "Haven't I shown you that we are all equal? Haven't I shown that the riches of the world must not be in the hands of gods?" He touched a hand to his breast, affecting a wounded look. "But there remain some among us who insist on worshipping the orisha, who insist on placing gods above man, who would hold us subservient to them."

"Boo!" someone cried.

"Death to believers!" another echoed.

"Death to sycophants!"

So *this* was why the orisha were growing weaker. Ashâke had felt a few orisha die. This was an attack, no longer from the shadows, whispering lies. They had come out in the open to unleash terror.

We need to get out of here, screamed Yemoja. *Now!*

"In the name of the Teacher," said Yaruddin.

"IN THE NAME OF THE TEACHER!" the crowd bellowed.

Ashâke watched with growing horror as Yaruddin stretched a hand to his side, as that terrible scimitar condensed into his fist. He raised the blade above his head. He was going to kill them. He was going to execute every one of them to send a message. And she couldn't just stand here and watch. She lurched forwards—

Don't even think about it. Get out of here!

The crowd seemed possessed, and Ashâke did not doubt that some of them were.

Ashâke had the sudden feeling of being watched. She cast around surreptitiously and—

There! She locked gazes with one of the guards standing in the shadow of the platform. The one with the single plait running down the middle of his head. He was staring unmistakably at her, brows creased as he put two and two together.

And then, recognition flashed in his eyes.

Ashâke's bowels loosened.

Run, you fool, bellowed Yemoja. *Run!*

Ashâke turned and cut through the crowd. She elbowed them, ignoring their protests, their curses, their bloodthirsty braying. Her scarf slipped and she clutched at it in desperation. Any moment now she expected to hear the guard give a cry, and oh it would be so easy to subdue her in this nest of vipers—

She broke free of the crowd, stumbled into the street, and knocked into something—some*one*. An *oof* escaped Ashâke's throat as they tumbled. Down and down she went, scraping her knees on the flagstones, before coming to a rest against a well. Ashâke sat up, mildly concussed. Opposite her the other person was extricating themself from the mess of tomatoes and palm kernels, clutching the ruins of a wicker basket as they turned to—

"*Simbi?*"

THREE

Ashâke gaped, unable to believe her eyes. "Stars above, it's you!"

Simbi looked older. But of course she *was* older. How many seasons had passed since she acceded? Five, six? It felt long. Too long. Still, Ashâke would always recognise those bushy eyebrows, those curious eyes, that mole just above her upper lip.

"Ashâke?" Simbi breathed. "Are my eyes deceiving me? What are you doing here?" She looked slowly from Ashâke to the square with the thundering crowd, and then back to Ashâke.

"I—"

Simbi sprang to her feet. "Hurry! We have to go."

And before Ashâke could utter a word Simbi seized her by the arm and steered her away.

They avoided the main thoroughfares, Simbi leading Ashâke down side streets and narrow alleys. She possessed a thorough knowledge of the city's secret paths, weaving through back streets, sometimes retracing her steps, constantly casting over her shoulder to ensure they were not being followed. Most of the city was at the square, save for the odd drunken loon, or the lame and blind who littered the alleys, and who paid Simbi and Ashâke no attention. Several times Ashâke tried to start up a conversation, but Simbi hushed her, and eventually she fell silent and allowed herself to be led, ignoring the gods' protests.

We can't trust her, said Yemoja. *How do we know she won't betray us?*

Ashâke ignored them. This was her friend, the reason she had come here, and she was only too glad to see her. She had never felt anything but safe in Simbi's presence. She didn't see why that should change now. They were friends, more than friends.

At last they entered a restaurant that proclaimed boldly over the lintel MAMA IBEJI'S FOOD JOINT and ascended a set of rickety stairs, and then Simbi was unlocking a door and ushering Ashâke into the room beyond.

"My home," said Simbi. "We should be safe here."

Simbi locked the door, hastened over to the windows, and bolted them shut, plunging the room into semidarkness. She vanished into the kitchen, returning moments later with a lantern that she settled gingerly on the table. Finally, she turned to Ashâke.

They stood some five strides apart, not speaking. They just . . . stared at each other. A dozen thoughts blazed through Ashâke's mind, a dozen things she wanted to say. But where should she start? How could one cram five seasons' worth of yearning and hoping and, ultimately, loneliness into mere words? Simbi had been her one friend, the person she had been closest to. And when she left . . . Ashâke hadn't been able to handle it. That, ultimately, was what drove her to build the idan, and set loose this cascade of events.

A metal cage hung from the rafters, rattling noisily as three pigeons fluttered about.

"You're hurt," said Ashâke. "Your . . . your cheek."

Simbi wiped a hand across her right cheek. "Tomato," she said. "A bloody tomato."

They burst into laughter. And just like that, they were back in the temple, giggling with nerves and fear and excitement from making it safely back to their room after a midnight jaunt, at having escaped Priestess Essie's hawk eyes. Ashâke closed the distance between them and threw herself into Simbi's open arms. And she couldn't say when her laughter turned to tears. And they were both laughing, and crying, spouting incoherent nonsense. But it was nonsense they understood, nonsense that expressed everything words could not contain, could not quantify. And when they'd spent themselves they knelt, arms thrown loosely about each other as they breathed quietly. Ashâke could feel Simbi's rapid heartbeats thudding against her chest.

"I've missed you," said Ashâke. "I've really, really missed you."

"Me too," said Simbi, her breath hot in Ashâke's ear. "You can't imagine how much. I . . . never thought I would see you again."

They remained locked in an embrace for what seemed like an eternity, and Ashâke wanted to freeze this moment, to cast it in bronze so that it endured for ever and ever. But she couldn't, and after a moment she pulled back from the hug, blinking tears from her eyes.

Simbi ran her hands over Ashâke's arms, gently tracing the godscript etched into Ashâke's skin. "You're an idan."

Ashâke gave a watery smile. What had taken her moons of research and stealing into the library, what, as Essie had remarked, even seasoned priests did not know, Simbi had deduced in a heartbeat. But then, she had always been clever.

"I know that look," said Ashâke, laughing. "You want to ask, so ask."

"Are they . . . with you right now?" asked Simbi. "The gods."

"They are always with me."

Simbi's eyes went round. "Can they . . . hear me?"

What a simpleton, Yemoja commented drily.

"Some of them can."

"What does it feel like?"

It felt as though she were being stretched at once in a thousand different directions. It felt as though she were carrying a dozen precious eggs and walking over a tight-rope, holding on to the crate lest she lose even one. It felt good, knowing that she had been chosen, that she was the only thing keeping the gods alive, safe. It felt maddening, comforting, isolating . . . "Indescribable," she said.

Simbi grinned. "I'm sure it is." And then, "I still can't believe it. Remember when you thought there was something wrong with you?"

"And those little shits would call me 'deaf priest,'" Ashâke laughed. "If only they could see me now."

"They're dead," said Simbi, sobering up. "All of them."

Ashâke's mouth went dry. "What?" she croaked.

"The godkillers found the temple. They killed the priests first, because they believed they knew you were the Guardian and would know of your whereabouts."

"But . . . they didn't!" cried Ashâke, aghast. "*I* didn't even know. Only Iyalawo—" Ashâke pushed to her feet and began pacing. "These godkillers. These . . . these *fucking godkillers!*"

"Keep your voice down!" cried Simbi, springing to her feet.

"You're right. I'm . . . I'm sorry. It's just—" She clenched her fists, unclenched them. "So many people dead. And . . . it's all because of me."

Because of us, said Yemoja. *And we're wasting time here.*

"Because you carry the orisha."

Ah, so she's not so simple after all.

"Have you ever faced a godkiller?" asked Ashâke. "They're not entirely human. Even the gods don't know what they are. But they're not human. Not anymore. Simbi, they can possess anyone, *become* anyone, do you understand what that means?"

"Scary . . ." said Simbi quietly. There was a strange look in her eyes as they slid towards the door. And . . . was it Ashâke's imagination or did her lips tremble? But then the thought of the godkillers would do that to anyone. "Why did you come here, Ashâke? Inysha is not safe, not for you."

From beneath her lashes, Ashâke looked shyly at Simbi. *I came for you,* she wanted to say. *We planned to get a house with a garden and I wanted to see you.* But instead she said, "I didn't expect to find the city like this, believe me. I wouldn't have come otherwise. What happened? The griots were supposed to be spreading the news that gods are alive. Instead I find the city—the *people* turned against the orisha. And who are the Ogboni?"

"A cult of godkiller worshippers," said Simbi, sitting next to her. "Humans who've renounced the orisha. They go about searching for anyone who still adheres to the old ways. Priests, acolytes, the small folk. The griots have scattered into the wild and anyone who even secretly still keeps an altar, or offers sacrifices . . . well, you saw what happened to those priests."

"Good gods," breathed Ashâke. "It's an all-out war."

49

Yemoja pronounced an oath. *Mortals,* she spat. *Vile, traitorous mortals.*

"I hear it's the same in other kingdoms," said Simbi. "The godkillers rarely show themselves. It is the people. It is *we* who have turned our backs on the gods."

"But why? I don't understand."

Simbi's eyes travelled to the door, absently fingering the pendant around her neck. "They offer eternal life. The chance to be gods."

"But that's impossible."

"They offer the chance to not die . . . like them."

Ashâke shuddered. They were making more godkillers? Leeches who'd simply seize bodies at will? That was a frightening notion.

"What about you, Simbi?" Ashâke asked. "Where do you stand? Are you for . . . or against the gods?"

Simbi gave a sad smile. "I am for myself, and the survival of my household."

Ashâke frowned. "Your household?"

"I have a family now. I have a chief husband and two lovely boys. Twins."

Ashâke felt suddenly lightheaded, as though the wind had been knocked out of her. She forced a smile, hoping Simbi could not sense her dismay. "A husband. Twins . . . I'm . . . I'm so happy for you." But was she? Was she really? But what had she expected? To find Simbi, waiting for her? Five seasons was a long time. And a lot could happen—a lot *had* happened—in that time. She could hardly fault Simbi for moving on with her life.

"Ibeji really showed you her favour."

Simbi's lips quivered in what might have been a smile. "Yes. Yes, she did." Her eyes slid towards the door.

"You keep glancing at the door."

"I do?" laughed Simbi.

"Yes, it's almost like you're expecting someone to burst through."

"Force of habit. It's what happens when you're living in the lion's den."

Any other person, and Ashâke would have chalked it up to that. But she knew Simbi, knew the way her lips trembled whenever she told a lie, knew the way her voice climbed just a little higher whenever she struggled to contain her emotions.

Ashâke glanced at the shoes by the door—children's shoes, and a large man's shoes—and saw clearly the fine coat of dust on them.

The room suddenly felt colder.

"Simbi," said Ashâke quietly, rising. "Where is your family?"

Simbi's eyes glistened with tears, and that was all the proof Ashâke needed.

"No," she breathed, slowly shaking her head. "No. Simbi what did you *do?*"

Simbi lunged at her. Ashâke yipped as she took the blow to her jaw. Pain. Bright, merciless pain bloomed across her face. She rocked backwards and hit the floor, stunned. Blood, thick and salty, filled her mouth. Ashâke moaned, struggling to focus, struggling against the darkness that seeped into the edges of her vision, that threatened to overwhelm her. She saw the pigeons flapping excitedly in their cage, saw the blackened rafters, saw Simbi straddling her as she fumbled a length of rope around Ashâke's wrists.

"Get off!" Ashâke mumbled. *"GET OFF!"*

With a roar she pushed Simbi. The woman went flying, skirts flapping as she crashed into the table. It collapsed beneath her weight. Ayò seeds emptied out of their pods, skittering across the wooden floor. The lantern crashed to the floor, chugging hot oil. A tongue of flame stretched from the wick and lapped up the oil, following its trail until it reached the curtains, which caught ablaze with a loud whoosh.

Ashâke wobbled to her feet, flinging away the rope. Her jaw stung where Simbi had hit her, her wrists burned from the rope. But none of that compared to the hurt in her heart, to the cold knowledge that Simbi had betrayed her, was trying to feed her to the godkillers.

"Why?" She gasped. *"Why?"*

"They have my family." Kohl-stained tears tracked a dark path down her cheeks. "The priests . . . they told the godkillers we were friends. Inseparable. They said—they said sooner or later you would come looking for me."

And she had come. Like a fool she had come to Simbi.

What did I tell you? said Yemoja. *I told you she couldn't be trusted!*

Simbi lunged again. But this time Ashâke was ready for her. She caught her in a headlock, and began to pound her back with her fist. Simbi tried to twist free of Ashâke's grip, she lost her footing, and then they were rolling on the floor where they grappled, clawing and snarling and biting. The result was an undignified tussle as each sought to gain the upper hand. Ashâke drove her knee hard into Simbi's belly. The woman folded in half, eyes bulging as the wind left her. Ashâke stumbled to unsteady feet, wobbled, and landed in a sprawl on the hardwood floor. Colourful lights exploded in her eyes. She shook the ringing from her ears, shook the lights dancing in her vision as she looked down to find Simbi clutching on to her ankle like a twice-cursed monkey.

"Let—go!" Ashâke yelled, struggling to shake her off. But Simbi's grip was true, fastened like a leech. "LET—GO!" She drove her other boot flat into Simbi's face. There was a satisfying crunch, the sickening give of bone.

Simbi let go, howling with pain. Ashâke scrambled to her feet. The room was on fire. Tall flames greedily licking every surface. She could hardly see for the smoke that choked the air. Overhead the pigeons were screeching in their cage.

Simbi rose. Her face was a ruin: eyes rapidly swelling shut, nose squashed and gushing blood. She clutched her belly, limping to block the door.

"Get out of my way," snarled Ashâke.

"They habh by bamily." Simbi grimaced, showing teeth turned red with blood.

"Can't you see the house is on fire? Do you want to die here?"

"Can'th leth you leab," Simbi wheezed, hands digging into her pouch. "I can'th—they'll be here thoon!"

Quick as an arrow she opened her palm and blew a fistful of something at Ashâke. A cloud of white dust filled the air and Ashâke gulped a lungful before she realised what was happening. The effect was instantaneous: the room flipped on its head, the flames turned to dancing fire wraiths.

"Uhhhh . . ." she groaned, stumbled backwards as the room swooned and her knees turned to water. She flailed, arms gasping desperately for purchase.

Simbi had filled her with a paralytic. She knew the herb all too well. Ba Fatai had given it to her whenever he wanted her to rest.

"I'm thorry." Simbi's voice came as if from the bottom of a well. Ashâke looked up at her, struggling to focus on that ruin of a face, one she knew and loved, one which had shared in her joy and pain. The stab of betrayal was acute. "I'm tho thorry," Simbi wept, her breath hot on Ashâke's face, snot and kohl-stained tears leaking down her oily cheeks. "They habh my pamily. I can'th . . . they habh my pamily."

It was hard to breathe. So hard. Ashâke could scarcely concentrate. She heard vaguely the panicked voices of the gods as they screamed at her to run. But she could not run.

She was on her knees now, wheezing as she crawled for the window.

BANG.

The door rattled in its frame as a series of blows came upon it.

"OPEN UP!" barked a coarse voice.

"Coming," Simbi piped up, scurrying through the inferno. Fresh terror gripped Ashâke. They were here. The godkillers were here.

Bang. Bang. *Bang.* "OPEN THIS FUCKING DOOR RIGHT THIS—"

The door exploded open.

No use hiding her powers. They were here; they knew she was here. Ashâke gathered the last of her strength and summoned the wind. A gust tore through the barricaded window, splinters flying free.

With a cry, Ashâke launched onto the sill and flung herself out the window. The last things she saw were Simbi's broken face and the shadows of three men barging into the room.

A Malady Most Strange

Yinka watched with increasing despair as Priest Lakunle performed the ritual. The small man muttered incantations as he waved a glowing incense stick over Enitan, who looked frail under the swathe of blankets. Yinka longed to be at his daughter's side, to hold her hand, to whisper words of comfort in her ear, but the priest had insisted he stay away. This was a warding ritual against evil and ailments, he had explained; the spirits that carried such ailments were always seeking something to attach themselves to, and Yinka would be a ready vessel if he remained in the room. So he watched instead from the living room, peering through the slit in the door. Reddish incense smoke stung his eyes and the back of his throat, but he did not shut the door.

Priest Lakunle was a priest of Shopona, lord of disease and maladies. When the strange illness had first taken Enitan, Yinka had consulted a witch doctor, but the woman's potions and salves did nothing to halt the progression of the disease, and eventually she advised that Yinka consult a priest of Shopona. "This is a strange malady," she had said. "Never seen anything of the sort."

The priest finished the ritual, gathered his things, and joined Yinka in the living room.

"Well?"

"The ritual is completed," said the priest, placing his bag on the low table. "Now we wait and see."

Yinka blinked. "Wait? *Wait?* How long must we wait? Until she—?" The words caught in his throat. "This is the twelfth warding in three moons—yes, I counted—and she's still no better!"

Priest Lakunle placed a gentle hand on his arm. "I understand your frustration, my son, I do. But Shopona—"

"He won't even take my offerings." Yinka shrugged off the priest's hand. "Why? Why won't he hear my prayers? *Why won't he respond?*"

"We can't always know the mind of the orisha."

"Then *what,* pray tell, is the point of you? What is the point of priests if you cannot intercede on our behalf—IF THE ORISHA WILL NOT ANSWER EVEN YOU!"

The priest shrank away from Yinka, eyes wide in alarm. He backed into the table, sending his bag crashing over, its contents skittering across the earthen floor. Yinka frowned, breathing hard. Then he saw that he was looming over the priest, arm upraised . . . as if . . . as if to strike him. "Oh." He backed away, overcome by a wave of shame. "Forgive me." He sank to his knees, bowing before the priest. "Forgive me. Please. I never . . ."

He burst into tears. It seemed to him that the tears came from nowhere. But he had kept his fears and doubts locked away for so long that now they simply bubbled over. Yinka had tried to hold himself together, to be strong for his daughter, to have faith. But how could one hold on to faith in the face of overwhelming despair? Yinka wept, snot and spit dribbling down his chin. He wept, hot tears stinging his eyes, until he was bawling, his body heaving with each wracking sob, a raw sound of anguish tearing out of his throat. He felt the priest's arms around him, and he melted into his embrace.

Yinka could not say how long they remained like that, how long he wept. But eventually his tears subsided and he peeled away from the priest, slightly embarrassed. "I've held you long enough," he said.

"I will continue my entreaties to Shopona," said Lakunle, as Yinka escorted him down the path away from his hut. "I will hold vigil for your daughter."

Yinka was no fool. He saw in the priest's eyes that there was nothing more to be done. Every rite had been performed. They could only wait and hope. Once, Yinka had carried Enitan into the river, where behind the curtain of a waterfall the priest had slaughtered a foal, invoking Shopona's mercy. Priest Lakunle had been sure the sacrifice would draw the attention of the orisha, that Shopona would come and remove the malady that afflicted his daughter. They had remained there for hours, shivering in the spray from the waterfall, and it wasn't until the golden rays of the sun split the sky that Lakunle had suggested they return home.

"Did I do something?" Yinka asked. "Did I offend the orisha? Am I being . . . punished?"

"Sometimes the orisha like to be courted. It is a test of your faith, of your devotion."

It was a clear night, and the sickle moon hung low in the sky. Hung so low Yinka felt if he stretched his hand he could almost touch it, climb the moon to Orun and confront Shopona . . .

But there *was* a way to get to Orun. Yinka wheeled to the east, where he could just make out the Tower, a needlelike structure from this distance, piercing the sky.

He could wait for the priest to continue his entreaties. But his daughter did not have much time and, frankly, he was done waiting.

"Baba? Baba!"

"Enitan!"

He dashed into the house, throwing open the doors with such force that they nearly flew off their hinges.

"Daughter," he gasped. "What is it?"

She stirred and he rushed to her side.

In the wan lantern light Yinka made out the huge scaly boils, each as large as a kola nut, that strained against her skin. Her skin that looked banana-leaf thin, stretched over the hard angles of her bones. The malady had consumed her eyes, several iridescent scales stretching over where they used to be. A mere three moons ago his Enitan had been a chubby child, her fast feet carrying her to the market and the warrens of the agboya cave where she hunted clamshells. Now . . . now she was little more than skin and bones, a shadow of herself who spent most of her time asleep.

The strange wasting disease had overrun the village. Several people had already perished from it. And yet, for some strange reason, not everyone fell to the disease. Though Yinka was no longer spry with youth he remained hale and hearty and unafflicted. And often, in the quiet hours of the morning when the cords of despair wound tight around his throat, he wept: *Take me instead. Take me and spare my Enitan.*

Enitan slept longer and longer, and Yinka feared that one of these days she might not wake. *Don't think that,* he chided himself. *May Olodumare take mercy on your wretched thoughts.* But it was hard not to think that way, when every day he watched, helpless, as she deteriorated, when Shopona remained silent and unheeding of his sacrifices and entreaties. As Yinka pulled back the blankets, he was overcome by a cloying fishy stench, but he didn't mind. And when he took her hands in his a boil burst open, foul-smelling pus seeping out of it. Yinka felt the sticky wetness in his hand, but he did not pull away; he held his daughter close, he held her tight, and he kissed her forehead. "My love. My light. I'm here."

"Father." Enitan's lips twitched in what he recognised as a smile. "I had a dream. The most wonderful dream!"

"You did?" said Yinka, mustering a false enthusiasm. "Tell me *all* about it."

"I dreamed I was a bird and I was flying. It was so beautiful. There were other birds and they told me to come. To join them."

Yinka bit his lips against a fresh outpouring of tears.

Nothing could have prepared Yinka for the sight of the Tower. It loomed, obliterating everything in sight, so that no matter which way he turned, the Tower was always in view—or rather, one's eye was always drawn towards the edifice. The grey-black exterior seemed endless, intricately etched with celestial script. Yinka felt small, insignificant, and he wondered how people could live in the shadow of such a structure.

Perhaps they've gotten used to it.

Ile-Ife itself was a wondrous city. The roads were wide and cobbled, the houses huge and sleek—a far cry from the adobe and wood shacks of his village. Several giant bronze statues lined the streets, and he recognised Oya and Yemoja and countless other orisha, caught in various imperious poses. Even the people seemed cleaner, their skin clearer, their clothes more colourful. Yinka had dreamed of one day moving to the capital—the first city in the world, where Obatala had cast his bowl of sand into the Endless Sea to create Aye—he had dreamed of bringing up his daughter in such a place, so she could study at the feet of learned scholars and better her mind. She was not going to be just the daughter of a tanner, but an exceptional scholar to rival the world's brightest.

Tears stung Yinka's eyes. He swallowed the lump in his throat. *I will do this for you, Enitan. I swear on my father's grave, I will.*

Yinka, who had been lurking by the inn's open patio, surreptitiously studying the Tower, looked up to find the innkeep hovering over him, a large drinking gourd and a cup at hand.

"Drink, my friend?"

"Eh, no. Thank you."

"Come on. I insist."

"I was just . . . I was just passing. Might I trouble you with a question, friend? How does one get in the Tower?"

The innkeep grinned, glanced at the Tower. "Like everyone else. Pick a blue stone."

Every season there was a Conclave of orisha and man. The Oba, his chiefs, and his priests would ascend the Tower to Orun, where they wined and dined with orisha. Select small folk, picked at random, were allowed to join the train.

Moons before the Conclave town criers went around with calabashes brimming with blue and black stones, and those who wished to visit Orun plunged their hands in hoping to pick a blue stone.

"I know that," said Yinka. He cast around, then said in a low voice, "But is there . . . no other way to get in there?"

The man gave him a very serious look, catching his meaning. "Ah . . ." He looked Yinka over. "Not from around here, are ya?" He swung a heavy hand onto Yinka's shoulder, then pointed with his cup. "See there, at the base of the Tawa. Those thingies that look like houses? There be guards in there. I lived here my whole life and I never see those guard posts abandoned. Well, friend, unless you can pull away those guards, there's no getting in the Tawa for you. Wait like the rest of us, and pick your blue stone, eh?" He hiccupped, considered Yinka anew. "What you want in there for anyway? To see the orisha? Speak to a priest or sumthin'."

At that moment someone bellowed "Ajala" and the man staggered away.

Yinka gritted his teeth. He hadn't really thought this through. He hadn't considered how he would get into the Tower. Obatala's breath, he hadn't imagined it to be so heavily guarded. But what did the orisha need guarding for anyway?

Another Conclave was fast approaching; the town criers would go out in half a moon. But Yinka had no intentions of waiting until then. What were the chances he would pick a blue stone? No. He had come this far. He couldn't, wouldn't, leave it up to chance.

His daughter could not afford the uncertainty of chance.

Yinka watched the inn burn. It had taken everything in him to light a torch and cast it into the thatch roofing. He hoped everyone got out.

"Come on," he muttered.

Just as he had hoped, the fires had created such commotion that the guards left their posts, running to help. Yinka nearly whooped with joy.

Heart pounding in his chest, he raced across the vast expanse towards the Tower. He kept expecting to hear a shout, to find guards racing after him, but miraculously, nothing happened. Surely this had to be a sign, an omen.

Reaching the grand Tower doors, he opened them and slipped into the darkness.

Two massive stone crucibles burned at the at the base of Orun's Gate, casting dancing shadows on the golden metalwork. A gate they said Ogun himself had made in his forge. Strange symbols were carved into the Gate, the language of the orisha, which seemed to move.

But the Gate, for all its magnificence, was not what

stopped Yinka in his tracks, was not what sent terror coursing through his heart.

Sitting cross-legged before the Gate was an orisha.

Not just any orisha. Eshu.

He sat with his back to Yinka, but where the back of his head should have been was a face. A terrible face full of wicked cunning. His eyes were black voids, save for fiery red irises, as though two rings of fire hung in a starless night sky. This was his new face. The story went that Eshu, ever the mischief-maker, had played a cruel trick on the Supreme Father. Olodumare, in his fury, gouged out Eshu's eyes and sewed shut his lips. Eshu, in turn, grew a new face. Bare of torso with a simple cloth around his loins, the lord of roads and crossroads seemed made of night.

Eshu slowly cocked his head to the side, a sly smile twisting his lips. "Why, my eyes do not deceive me. It is, indeed, a mortal at the Gate of Orun."

Yinka wondered how he must look to the orisha. A gnat, an insignificant thing. He stood, petrified, unable to tear his eyes away from Eshu. And it seemed to him that the orisha held him spellbound, *made* him look into those terrible eyes. The silence stretched on for what felt like seasons—

"Are you mute?"

Yinka swallowed. "I . . . I was not expecting . . . anyone here at the Gate."

"No?" Eshu sounded amused. "Am I not the lord of roads and crossroads? Am I, Eshu Elegba, not the god of gates and pathways? Do I not hold the hidden paths in the palm of my hand? Is this, mortal, not a Gate?"

Yinka dropped to his knees and pressed his forehead to the ground. "My lord," he gasped, heart thudding in his hears. "Mighty, powerful Eshu. I meant no disrespect. Forgive this idiot mortal."

Yinka squeezed his eyes shut and balled his fists to still his trembling hands.

"Look at me."

Slowly, Yinka raised his head and gazed at the orisha.

"Why are you here?"

"I—my daughter. She's sick. I fear . . . I fear she'll die. I'm here to petition Shopona."

"There are priests for that."

"The priests have failed and I don't know what else to do. I am at my wit's end."

Eshu slowly turned his head; he rotated his neck until his second face was turned away, and the first one was facing Yinka. This one was even more hideous. Where the eyes should be were two ruined and mottled orifices, and his lips were sewn shut with a copper thread. "So you have come all this way. Why not ask me to deliver your petition?"

Eshu was also messenger-lord of the orisha.

"I would see him myself . . . if it please you."

Eshu was silent for so long that Yinka began to fear he had offended him. Then he waved a hand. "Go on, then. See my dear brother for yourself."

With an earthly groan the Gate swung open.

"Thank you," said Yinka.

His footfalls echoed across the space as he approached Eshu. As he walked past, he couldn't resist looking up at the god, and he found Eshu's head turning, those terrible eyes watching him.

Eshu was smiling.

FOUR

It was a long way down.

At least it seemed so. Ashâke fell, flipping head over heels, the wind screaming in her ears. Simbi had betrayed her. Simbi had *betrayed* her. She should have listened to the gods and stayed away, but she had been clinging on to a memory, an idea of Simbi that no longer existed. The loving friend, the one who would jump into fire, who would take lashings for her, was long gone. And now because of her bullheadedness, because she had not listened to the orisha, she was plunging to certain death and she was taking the orisha with her. The gods screamed in her mind, but Ashâke could scarcely make sense of what they were saying. She didn't need to. She felt their panic, their fear. Ashâke wanted it all to be over. All she needed do was close her eyes and wait for death to claim her.

She landed on something soft—the awning of the downstairs restaurant. It flung her into the air like a catapult, and when she crashed back into it, there was a sharp ripping sound as the cloth tore. The poles that propped it up snapped under the stress, and Ashâke tumbled to the street in a tangle of sheet and ropes and broken poles.

She groaned, untangling herself. A blast of evening air hit her, rife with the stink of fire and burning wood. Three paces away a boy stared curiously at her as he sucked his thumb. He looked from the window back to her, and a grin slowly spread across his face.

"Fly," he said.

Ashâke staggered to her feet, nearly blacked out from the sudden movement—

A scream pierced the night. Ashâke whipped around, searching for the source, and there! She locked eyes with a cane-weaver across the street, pointing as she screeched her heart out.

"No," said Ashâke, batting her hands as though swatting flies. "No, don't scream."

Raised voices. The woman's bellows had drawn attention, and Ashâke saw several figures pour into the street, bronze and leather armour glinting in the inferno. Guards. The godkillers had brought friends.

"There!"

"There she is!"

"SEIZE THE GUARDIAN!"

At that moment the upstairs apartment exploded, sending pieces of timber and plaster flying through the night. With an almighty groan, what remained of the building began to crumble.

And though in that moment her anger at Simbi filled every fibre of her being, Ashâke found herself wondering if—*hoping* that she had made it to safety, that she hadn't perished in the fire.

Pandemonium reigned: people scattered, running helter-skelter as they sought to distance themselves from the inferno. Ashâke dived into the din of the chaos.

Everything hurt. Good gods, everything hurt. Her left leg was completely numb, and it dragged as she raced down the street, a useless log of wood. Still, she ran. She could not afford to get caught. But it seemed more and more likely that she would. Already she could feel the paralytic stealing over her body. And it was only a matter of time before she keeled over, frozen and helpless, a ready offering for the godkillers.

A spider burst out of the street ahead. Large as an elephant, the beast scuttled towards Ashâke with alarming speed, legs clicking on the flagstones. Where its head should be was Simbi's head, in her mouth a row of sharp teeth, eyes black as midnight as she yelled, "They habh my pamily!"

Ashâke screamed, diving out of the way to find it was nothing more than a rickshaw, wheels squeaking as it barrelled down the street.

Yeoleaf was not only a potent paralytic but a powerful mind-altering herb. And it was already conjuring up her worst nightmares.

"Not real," she told herself, wiping the sweat from her forehead. "It's not real—"

A vise grip clamped around her arm. Someone whipped her around so violently that the world spun. But Ashâke fought the blackness seeping into the edges of her vision, fought the bile bubbling up her throat, as her eyes focused on the frowning face of a guard.

"No," she gasped. She recognised him. He had been in the square, at the execution. He was the guard who had recognised her.

"Come with me, Guardian," he growled, and began dragging her up the street.

He was strong. Gods, he was so strong. And she might have fought him off, but her limbs were already locking. Ashâke felt disoriented, oddly disembodied, as though she were merely observing the scene from somewhere above. And she watched with terror and utter helplessness as the guard hauled her up the street.

"What's the matter with you?" he spat. "Get up! Now!"

Her etchings began to glow. She called the wind. A surge of power coursed through her and for a moment the world grew bright. Everything was clear. And she was not afraid.

A look of alarm crossed his eyes. "Wait—!"

A gust blasted through the alley. It took the guard full in the chest and sent him flying. He crashed into the wall, then slid to the ground where he remained unmoving, a trail of dark red blood smearing the grimy wall.

Good, said Yemoja. *Now run.*

Ashâke ran. But her legs were bronze casts and would not move. She tripped and fell. The ground rushed up to meet her, and the world went black.

Ashâke was aware of a bitter taste in the back of her throat as she came to. She opened her eyes to darkness. The ground beneath her was uneven and cold, and somewhere in the dark came the steady drip . . . drip . . . drip of water into a puddle. She was thirsty. So thirsty. She ached all over. She felt as though she had been pummelled. Why did she hurt as—

And then it all came flooding back. Simbi's betrayal, the fire, throwing herself out the window, fleeing from the guards. She would have escaped, had it not been for the paralytic.

"She wakes!" crowed Arewa, lord of beauty and debauchery, from somewhere in the dark. "The queen rouses from slumber. Praise be!"

"Where are we?" Her mouth tasted of soot and old blood.

"Why, in your very own palace, my liege."

Ashâke's eyes were now adjusting to the dark and she made out a rectangle where the darkness was lighter, interrupted by darker vertical strips. Iron bars. "We're in a dungeon."

"Attagirl."

Ashâke could not shake the irony that she had been locked up in a similar manner at the temple. There was an awful stink to the air. Ashâke thought it the excrement of previous prisoners, but it smelled worse.

"No. *Foolish* girl." Yemoja's voice rang with cold fury.

At that moment there came a loud sound, as of metal grating against stone. Then, heavy footfalls. Light appeared somewhere to the right, searing the darkness. It grew steadily the closer the footfalls came, illuminating the wet, pockmarked floor and the black water beyond it. A canal. Her prison was right on the lip of a canal.

Her jailer came into view.

It was the guard, the one who had seized her in the street. He bore in one cloth-wrapped hand a lantern, whose dancing flames threw his face into sharp relief, so that he seemed for one moment like a carved block of wood. The left side of his face was covered in dark dried blood from a terrible gash in his temple. Probably where he had hit his head. On his neck, inked across the skin beneath a rough stubble, was a jackal-head tattoo that marked him as an Ogboni.

"You're awake. Good." He had a gravelly voice, one that would not seem out of place in a dark alley, whispering quiet threats into frightened ears. He reached into his pockets; when Ashâke shrunk backwards, he paused. "I mean you no harm."

"You've locked me in a cage," she said.

He grimaced, fumbled for a key that he began to rattle in the lock. "I couldn't leave you lying in the street. And I had to lead the others away." The door creaked open, and he offered a large hand. "Come with me. I'll help you out of the city."

Ashâke frowned. Was this some kind of trick? She had learned the hard way to trust no one, more so a guard pretending to be her friend. More so an Ogboni. Something was not right.

"We must hurry," he said, his obvious impatience turning his voice coarser. "It won't be long before they notice I'm gone."

"Your fellow Ogboni?"

His face spasmed, as though he had tasted something sour. "I'm not one of them."

"No? Your proud tattoo begs to differ. I've played the fool once this night already—"

Voices above.

He seized her by the arm. "Come!"

"I don't—trust you!" hissed Ashâke, yanking herself free.

He gaped at her as though she had lost her wits. "Who the fuck asked for your trust? Do you want to live or not?"

The voices were getting closer now. Flickering firelight appeared in the distance. "I'll find my own way," she said, and started in the opposite direction.

The guard swore, and grabbed her for the third time that night, slamming her against the wall. There was something feverish in his eyes as he hissed, "You won't. They have eyes everywhere, don't you see? The only way to trick them is to be one of them. To be a part of the thousand-and-one eyes of Bahl'ul's followers."

He glanced hastily in the direction of the approaching voices. "Now, you may choose to go on your way, but you won't make it very far. You certainly will never reach the gates. And all this will have been for nothing." He watched Ashâke with keen eyes as she digested his words. "You could also try to fight. Although something tells me you wouldn't be running if you could take the godkillers. Which leaves you one option. Come with me. I'm not asking for your trust—only fools trust without thinking. But for the moment our agendas align, and that is enough for me."

Either he was a spy, a secret worshipper who had managed to infiltrate the ranks of the Ogboni, or he was pretending to be one. But to what end? Why would he choose to help her if he could simply hand her over to the godkillers? There was no time to think about it. The moment they were out of the city she would make a run for it. "Fine," she told the guard. "Lead the way."

Ashâke hurried after him, struggling to keep pace with him. As they turned the bend, he smashed the lantern, quenching the flames, then tossed it into the water. He held her and pressed into an alcove, a hand over her mouth. They were so close together she could smell the sweat on his skin, could feel the thump of his heartbeat. It was, miraculously, steady.

"Ugh, this place stinks." A high reedy voice. "Why's it always us getting the worst jobs, eh?"

"You never shut your fucking mouth, that's why."

"Me? That's no fair! I asked if we could go home. Only right seeing as our shift was ended. You know my wife is cooking ewa agoyin for dinner. And I like it hot."

"Was a stupid thing to ask. The Guardian is at large. Did you think we were just going to go home?"

Reedy Voice's belly gave an audible rumble.

"Couldn't have waited till tomorrow to show herself. 'S not like she's down here anyway. Guaaaardiaaaan!" sang Reedy Voice playfully. "Are you there?" His girlish titters echoed through the tunnel. "Come out, come out. In the name of the Teacher, I command you show your—!"

A sharp thwack.

"Ow! What did you hit me for?"

"Cuz you're stupid."

"*You're* stupid."

"Can't be saying his name anyhow."

"What, the Teacher?"

Another sharp smack.

And they carried on bickering as their voices and footfalls faded away.

Humanity's finest and brightest, said Arewa cheerfully. *This is what the orisha fell to.*

"They're gone," said the guard. "Come."

He peeled away from the alcove and Ashâke stumbled

after him, blind as a mole. The guard blundered on without hesitation and she wondered how he could see. But then, he must be familiar with these tunnels. Just as Ashâke's eyes began to adjust to the dark, making out the vast curved ceiling of the tunnel, and the even blacker water, he jumped into the water.

"What are you—oh . . ." Bobbing low in the canal was a canoe, its gunwales so wide and low it resembled a raft.

"Get in."

Ashâke jumped. She landed too hard and too far and the canoe tipped to the right, dancing precariously beneath their combined weight. Ashâke gasped as cold water rushed in, arms flapping as she struggled to keep from splashing into the water. She heard the guard curse behind her, and just when she thought the canoe would flip over and dump them both in the water, he wrapped a strong arm around her waist and yanked her back to the middle.

"I'm not looking to take a bath," he said, taking the oar. "Nor am I looking to explain why I'm wet as a dog when I return to the others."

"You're going back?"

"Of course."

He waited until she was seated, then began to row quietly.

"What is this place?" she asked as they reached a juncture where several tunnels met.

"Flood tunnels," he grunted. "Keeps water out of the city, for when the sea rushes in at high tide."

That made sense. Inysha meant "the city on the sea," in truth built on an outcropping of rock that overlooked the Endless Sea.

"So . . . why are there cells down here if it floods over?"

"To drown criminals. Cutthroats and cutpurses. Lock 'em down here and wait for high tide."

Ashâke regarded the walls, the wet, vaulted tunnel ceiling. How must it feel to watch the water slowly rise, to float to the top until there was no more air to be drawn? She shuddered. A truly bad way to go. She wondered what sick mind had designed such cells.

The guard's back rippled as he paddled. And she wondered how he could turn his back to her. Wouldn't it be prudent to have her sit in front, where he could keep her in sight? It was either that he trusted her—but then, he had made it clear what he thought about that—or that he did not fear her, did not believe she could overpower him.

"I saw you, at the execution. Why did you come here?"

A pang of sorrow at the thought of Simbi, who had asked her the very same question. "Chasing a ghost."

He grunted.

Simbi had betrayed her, given her up to save her family. And though it hurt to think about it, Ashâke understood. They were friends . . . had *been* friends, but blood ran thicker than water. What would it say about Simbi if she readily turned her back on her husband and children, if she abandoned them to help her? Ashâke did not know that she would want that kind of a person as a friend, or that she would be comfortable with the idea. And yet . . . she could not push from her mind the image of Simbi trying to subdue her, nor stop herself from envying the fervour with which she had fought for her family—a fervour and devotion that had once exclusively been Ashâke's. She mourned the loss of what they had had, of what could have been, and cursed the cruel godkillers.

A patch of lighter darkness appeared ahead. Ashâke could taste the brine in the air, and the chill that blew in from the sea. The guard pulled the canoe to the side behind a boulder and helped her up onto the cliff. White waves broke against the boulders. Freezing salt spray hit Ashâke and she shivered.

"Go to Abeokuta," he said. "It is the one city that has not fallen to godkillers, or the Ogboni. You will be safe there."

"How hasn't it fallen?"

"Easy. They keep their gates locked. No one goes in, no one goes out, lest a godkiller possess one of them. There is a census every morning and night so everyone is accounted for."

So they were under voluntary siege. Ashâke wondered how long that would last. She considered the quite obvious possibility that godkillers were already in the city, had been in the city long before they thought to lock themselves in.

He shrugged, seeing her expression. "You know more

than anyone you can't be too careful when dealing with a faceless adversary."

"Well, I suppose I should thank you . . . for helping me."

"Djola," he said suddenly.

"What?" said Ashâke, confused.

"You asked why I was helping you. I'm helping you because of Djola."

"How do you know . . . *Oh* . . ."

Of course! Of course, how could she have missed it? Where Djola had been slim and fluid as a blade of grass, this man was huge and barrel-chested; where Djola had had an easy smile, this man was all hard planes and scowls, brimming with a quiet menace. But for all their differences there was no mistaking the determined set of his jaw, the coal-black eyes, the proud nose. He looked like an older, hardened version of the griot who had silently crept up on her six moons ago, who had first offered her food and drink and a place at the fire.

"You're his brother."

He nodded, but made no move to row away. His throat stone bobbed up and down, and he looked like he was struggling with something.

"Tell me, Guardian." The words tumbled from his lips as though he feared if he stopped he wouldn't be able to say them. "Is he still alive . . . is he in there somewhere?"

"I . . ." Was that why he stayed in the Ogboni? Was he clinging on to hope that beneath skin and sinew his brother was in there? Ashâke couldn't imagine what torture it must be for him, to look in Djola's face day and night and wonder. She wished she could tell him what he wanted to hear, allay his worries. But instead, she said, "I—I don't know . . . I'm sorry . . ."

He shut his eyes and inhaled slowly. For a moment Ashâke thought he was fighting back tears, but when he opened his eyes, they were dry. In the moonlight he looked so much like Djola, who had crept up on her as she watched the griots, wishing to be among their number. Djola, who had played Jagu-Jagu with Ralia and the other children. Djola, who had come to her aid twice to rescue her from Yaruddin, paying the ultimate price. A familiar pang of guilt twisted her insides.

You know, said Arewa. *It occurs to me that this fine fellow is not helping Ashâke because she is the Guardian. Or because of us, no—no. Here is not a man so overcome with fervour, so seized with inspiration as to save his orisha. He is simply . . . trying to save his brother. What does that say?*

Shut your mouth, fool, snapped Yemoja. *Sometimes I wish you perished in the Fall.*

Arewa affected a gasp of horror—*Mother!*—then fell silent.

"Do you know Ralia?" asked Ashâke.

"That little fox." Was it her imagination or did his voice soften?

"How is she?"

"Being a handful. She's commandeered the other rascals to thwart the Ogboni at every turn. They've gotten very good at slipping in and out of places. Tearing down drawings of you, and putting out sacrifices to the orisha in public places." He shook his head. "Dangerous. But she won't listen."

Ashâke could not help but feel a swell of pride. Ralia, like all the other children, like Djola's brother, had lost a lot at the hands of the godkillers, and this little act of defiance, of bare-faced rebellion, gave her hope. Still, a tinge of worry soured her pride. The godkillers were ruthless, and Ashâke held no illusions about what would become of Ralia if ever she was caught.

"Will you . . . send her my . . ." The guard waited patiently, watching her in that keen way of his as she fumbled for words. "Just—tell her to be careful."

He scoffed. "I'd have more luck asking the sun not to shine." The guard turned away, clambered into the canoe, and began to row.

"Wait," she called. "What is your name?"

He was already vanishing into the black of the tunnel when he called, "Djábri."

"I'm Ashâke!"

The darkness swallowed him, and it was as though he had never been there in the first place.

FIVE

Djábri was just pushing closed the grate that led to the tunnels when a voice piped up behind him.

"There you are. Where've you been?"

The voice belonged to Leaf, a lower guardsman. He had been down in the tunnels with Quadri, complaining loudly about his ewa agoyin. He had large froggy eyes, buckteeth, and a rash spattered across his neck. Djábri could never remember his name; everyone called him Leaf, on account of his lanky form, and he, in turn, answered to it.

Djábri glowered at him. "Are you asking me questions?"

"No, no! I was just looking for . . . Oya's tits—wha' *happened* to your face? Did you . . . oooh"—Leaf's eyes went round—"you met her, didn't—?"

Djábri pushed past him. Leaf squawked as he sprawled onto his ass.

"What did you do that for?" he called, and when Djábri didn't answer, yelled, "Yaruddin's asking for you!"

Djábri's heart stopped cold. He whipped around. "What?"

"Yeh. Wants to see you. And I been running all over the city looking for you." Then he added, more to himself, "My ewa agoyin is definitely cold now."

"Did he say why?"

"Didn't ask." He chuckled nervously, scratching at his rashes. "You know no one asks him questions, Captain."

The thousand-and-one eyes of the godkillers. Djábri wouldn't be surprised if he had been found out, if somehow they knew he had helped the Guardian. In the beginning, when Yaruddin and his cohort had taken over the city, they had known just which people kept altars to the orisha in their homes. For the life of him Djábri had never been able to deduce how they had known, but he had developed a healthy terror of them ever since, a healthy paranoia. For one mad moment he contemplated fleeing back into the tunnels. The canoe was still there. He could paddle out of Inysha and flee to Abeokuta where the resistance was huddled. But . . . no. He had been careful. He hadn't risen through the ranks of the Ogboni to run now.

He couldn't leave without his brother.

"Where is Yar?"

There were nine courtyards in the palace, one for each level of the sprawling court. It was said Oba Adeniji, who had been a worshipper of the sky-orisha Obatala, had commanded the construction of the courtyards in such a manner so wherever he was he could look at the sky and commune with his orisha. That had been nearly a thousand seasons ago, before the making of the Tower.

Djábri stepped into the ninth courtyard, the largest and topmost one, which overlooked the city below. A gust of wind stirred through the yard, bringing with it a smell of sweet rot. It came from the iroko tree that grew near the centre of the yard. The massive tree's powerful roots dug into the limestone floor, sending cracks spidering across the white tiles. Soon the entire floor would be a network of cracks giving way before the roots. *Like the godkillers,* Djábri thought, *tearing into every facet of our lives.* As he passed under the tree he had the sudden feeling of being watched and he glanced up, half expecting to find Yar perched on a limb, peering at him in that disconcerting way of his. But there was nothing and no one there. Just gnarled limbs sagging under the weight of swollen fruits.

By some failure of construction the yard was without a wall so that it dropped cleanly into open air. And it was here, at the very lip of the yard, that Yaruddin stood, his back to Djábri, as he surveyed the city below. It was a dizzying drop, and for the briefest moment, Djábri considered sneaking up to Yaruddin and pushing him off the edge. Could he fly? He was never sure what the godkillers were capable of—Yaruddin in particular. But if he somehow managed to catch Yaruddin off guard, if the godkiller somehow perished in the drop, then so would his brother.

Djábri stopped ten paces from Yaruddin and cleared his throat. The skies to the east were beginning to lighten. It had been a long night, and Djábri couldn't shake the feeling that the day to come would be even longer.

"What news of the Guardian?" asked Yaruddin.

"I fear . . . I fear she has slipped away, my lord."

"Hmm. She has gotten very good at slipping away. I had her in my grasp, several moons ago. But this was before I knew she was the Guardian. And when I realised, well . . . but you know all this, don't you, Captain?"

"Beg pardon?"

"Surely you've heard the Songs?"

Djábri licked his lips. He had been on guard duty at the palace when Ashâke had come with the children, and she had left before he returned from his weeklong shift. But his ma had told him everything, including the fact that Djola was dead. He had watched her make the Song, and when she was done, he had experienced the details of that wretched day. He had seen the moment Djola died . . . only for his brother to stride into the city weeks later, turning the world on its head. "The griots Sing no more. We made sure of that."

Yaruddin turned.

Djábri drew in a sharp breath. He would never get used to it. To seeing his brother before him. And yet knowing that it wasn't truly his brother. It made no sense. But he could not show any emotion, could not afford to have Yaruddin suspect him, so he arranged his face into an expression of polite blankness.

The godkiller was staring at the gash on his temple, at the patina of dried blood on his cheek.

"I ran into the Guardian," Djábri explained. "She . . . she attacked me. It is a miracle I'm alive."

Yaruddin's black eyes lingered for a moment on the wound. He was so close Djábri could feel the heat rising off his skin, could see the pores on his nose. "Do you know, Captain, when the Guardian invokes her powers, we can feel it? Yes, there is this connection that always draws us to her . . . like moths to a flame. Tonight, she invoked her powers. I rushed to the street, naturally, but she was nowhere to be found." A pause. "And neither were you."

Slowly, slowly, Yaruddin looked into Djábri's eyes.

He knows, thought Djábri, his heart thrashing in alarm. *He knows what I've done.* But Djábri remained utterly still. He held Yaruddin's eyes, no matter how much he wanted to look away. He kept his face blank as he struggled to quell his growing panic .

"She summoned the wind." Djábri was surprised at the steadiness of his voice. "Tossed me far away. I passed out—"

"YARUDDIN!" bellowed a voice behind him.

Djábri whipped around, flipping his spear in the same movement and pressing the tip into the neck of the newcomer.

Before him stood a middle-aged, balding man, dressed in flowing black agbada. A gold earring dangled from his left ear, and his skin was the rich ebon of one who had spent a lifetime labouring in the sun. He looked in contempt from the spear at his neck to Djábri.

"Turn that spear away from me, boy," he said, "before you do something you will regret."

Djábri bristled. But there were very few people in the world who would dare barge in here, yelling Yaruddin's name in such manner.

"It's alright, Captain," said Yaruddin. "Leave us."

"My lord."

Djábri withdrew his spear, bowed to Yaruddin, and walked stiffly away. He could hear his blood rushing in his ears, feel his heart thrashing in his chest. *Dead gods. Great, dead gods.* How close, how so very close he had come to being eviscerated. That godkiller could have simply run him through with his scimitar, and it would have all been over. He would be turned to a statue, and his ma would lose another son. But instead he had chosen to waste words on him. Djábri was thoroughly shaken. It had been a long night, and he wanted to curl up in bed.

But this man was a new face, and he had barged in here yelling Yaruddin's name. Djábri had to know why. He glanced over his shoulder, saw that he was far from Yaruddin and the newcomer, then slipped behind a massive ornamental vase, crouching until he was hidden in the bushes.

"Vashek," he heard Yaruddin say. "I was not expecting you."

"Just *what* do you think you are doing?" snarled Vashek.

"I'm afraid I'm at a loss—"

"Don't play the fool, Yaruddin. You know *exactly* what I'm talking about."

"Well, the Guardian is in town, didn't you hear? I am merely trying to ferret out a rat. Sometimes the best course of action is to set a fire and wait."

"And you would burn the whole world to catch one rat."

"Well, the rat in question is a big one."

"Regardless." Vashek leaned close, lips peeled back in menace. "Public executions, guards running all over the city. Recruiting—*mortals?* Have you lost your wits? Have you forgotten that we work from the shadows?"

"We have worked from the shadows, Vashek. Where did that get us? How many of the followers are there—two hundred? Three hundred? There aren't enough of us to do the work that needs be done. But with the Ogboni—"

"The Teacher has a grand design."

"Then share it with me. Tell me what it is, brother, so I can serve." A pause. "Unless . . . you are not privy to this design?" Vashek's nostrils flared, and Yaruddin's eyes widened with wicked glee. "That's it, isn't it? Even *you* don't know!"

"I never said that," snapped Vashek.

"Tell me, Vashek. *Where* is the Teacher?"

"That is not for you to know. I did not come here to answer your questions. You will answer mine." He stepped closer. "You have removed obas and installed followers in their place. You have ignored every one of my dispatches to you—made *me* come all the way down here. If I didn't know better, I would say you seek to rule the Ten Kingdoms."

A tense moment passed. In which fire spat and crackled in the crucible. In which the yard grew considerably chillier. Djábri could feel an energy in the air, a strange power not unlike what he had felt before the Guardian summoned the wind.

They appeared. Djábri couldn't have said from whence they came. One moment Yaruddin and Vashek were alone in the yard; the next two dozen figures peeled from the shadows. They ranged from a youth around Ralia's age, to an old woman with silver-grey hair near the pillared entrance. But there was no mistaking who they were. They were, all of them, older than the skins they wore. Djábri could not say he had ever seen that many godkillers in one place. It frightened him.

Vashek looked slowly around. And the godkillers watched him silently, watched him with black, unblinking eyes, watched him watch them.

"You wayward followers of Bahl'ul," he sneered. "Have you all forgotten that I am the First of the Followers? *Do you really think you can take me?*"

"Go back to Skaggás, Vashek." Yaruddin's voice oozed a quiet menace. "To your little shop, and your little figurines."

Vashek turned back to Yaruddin, and his eyes burned with anger. He looked like he would say something, but then he spun about on his heels and stalked down the yard.

For one mad moment Djábri thought they would attack, like hounds at a prey, but the moment passed, and Vashek was sweeping out of the yard, his agbada billowing behind him.

SIX

"It doesn't look like anyone's here," said Ashâke, squinting. "It looks . . . abandoned."

The caravansary lay some five hundred paces in the distance, a collection of smaller baked brick buildings attached to the main one by walkways. They were bleached the colour of sand by the unrelenting sun. A sun which now beat down on Ashâke and made the air shimmer. She squinted, putting up a hand to shield her eyes. The caravansary had fallen into decay, and it looked, well, abandoned. Once, as Arewa had remarked, merchants from Ibis and Yarro and Sapele in caravans laden with cane sugar, palm oil, casks of palm wine—sometimes the rare and coveted crocodile leather—would stop here on their way to Abeokuta or Akure, which lay to the far east; but this was no longer an oft-travelled route, not for many seasons. The majestic walls were crumbling under the rot and neglect; the main house was caved in.

"We keep moving," said Yemoja, turning away.

"I can't go on any longer," said Ashâke. "I really can't. I might be the Guardian, but I am still human, and I need to rest."

The goddess's eyes burned.

"You could force me to go on, but sooner rather than later I will drop from exhaustion. And . . . you don't want me to pass out in the middle of the desert, do you?" she said. "That would leave me vulnerable . . ."

Ashâke had a point, and she could see on Yemoja's face that she knew this, and there was nothing she could do. The goddess scowled even deeper.

Another reason for you to be angry at me, Ashâke thought. The goddess was furious at her, had been furious at her ever since Inysha. But, quite uncharacteristically, she hadn't said a word, perhaps because of their flight. Ashâke could feel her displeasure, though, a roiling thing that tasted of ash and brine. But that was a problem for another time. How could she have known Inysha had been overrun by godkillers? How could she have known Simbi would betray her?

If she had to take one more step in this blasted desert she would wither from exhaustion.

"Fine. We rest here a few hours."

Ashâke had been on the road for nearly three days. First running, then walking, stopping only very briefly to rest before she was roused by the gods to keep moving. At first she had had no problem with it, egged on by a healthy dose of fear and a desperate need to put as much distance as she could between her and Inysha. Half the time she expected to find godkillers hot on her heels, Djábri in tow, having given her up. But she saw neither godkillers nor Djábri, and the sharp edge of terror soon blunted, returned to the constant undercurrent that had bubbled in the back of her mind ever since she learned she was the Guardian. She'd relaxed a little and, no longer spurred by the rush of flight, a stark weariness came over her.

The truth was, Ashâke was tired of running. So tired. The truth was, she was exhausted. She wanted nothing more than to curl up in a ball and sleep. Perhaps for a thousand seasons. To wake up and find that it was all over.

Worse was the thought of Simbi. The thought of her would come at the oddest of hours, and Ashâke would feel anew the sting of betrayal. And on the heels of that, an overwhelming mix of anger and sorrow. Anger at the godkillers, and sorrow at the choice Simbi had been forced to make, choosing her family over Ashâke. But Ashâke knew firsthand that there were no bonds stronger than those of the blood. Hadn't her own mother brazenly risked the wrath of the gods, locking them away so she could keep *her* safe, to protect *her* from this very situation, this endless constant danger?

The truth was, they were no closer to finding any answers. Not about the godkillers or where they got their powers or even why they wanted the orisha dead. A full six moons of chasing ghosts and they had come up with nothing. Well, except for the strange not-metal, which the farahàn had given them in Ile-Ife. Ashâke reached into her pouch for it.

She frowned. Her hand brushed her waterskin. She rooted through her pouch, her blood coursing in her ears, praying, hoping, that it was in there somewhere. She could not panic. She could not let the orisha see her panic. But there was no cause for alarm, she told herself. The rock had to be somewhere. She searched through the inner pockets of the pouch. Her dagger, a piece of dried bread, her flaccid waterskin folded into the bare interior of the pouch.

The object was gone.

The object was gone. She tried to think when last she had seen it. In Ile-Ife? No, she had taken it out after that. Before they entered Inysha? But she had had her pouch with her. Which meant it was somewhere in the city. She thought back to the crowd, the rabid Inyshini at the execution. Had a pickpocket slipped their hand into her pouch? Had she lost it as she tussled with Simbi? Oh gods, it could be anywhere. At Simbi's house, in the tunnels beneath the city. *Anywhere.*

Their only piece of a clue and she had lost it.

"Ashâke," called Oya, jolting her from her reverie. "What's the matter?"

"I . . . nothing," said Ashâke, hoping her smile did not betray her thrashing heart. "I just . . . need to rest."

Just as she could feel their emotions, in the same way they could feel hers.

"What is it?"

"Nothing."

"Ashâke. Do not lie to me."

"I'm just . . . exhausted."

"You poor dear." Oya's face softened. She took Ashâke by the hand. The gods were already making their way towards the caravansary. "Come."

Moonlight was streaming through the high window of the small room when Ashâke woke up. Eshu was staring at her.

Scattered across the caravansary were various effigies of Eshu. They ranged from small bronze statuettes to giant sculptures of the orisha. They were all the same, Eshu seated cross-legged with one terrible face looking forwards, the other looking backwards, for though he was messenger-lord of the orisha, he was also lord of roads and crossroads, and his eyes were all-seeing.

Travellers often placed sacrifices to Eshu by the roadside, at crossroads, and at caravansaries, that he may guide the path. Every caravansary strewn across the Ten Kingdoms was dedicated to him.

A curious feeling overcame Ashâke as she gazed at the statue. It was, in a way, the very same image she had built what felt like a lifetime ago—albeit devoid of the godscript that would make it an idan. Ashâke knew all the gods she carried with her: Oya, Ogun, Arewa, and Yemoja, the four strong enough to manifest; and the countless others who were so weak that they slumbered, clinging on to life by waning will. But Eshu, messenger god, lord of roads and crossroads, master of mischief, was not with her. He was dead, like countless other gods, slaughtered in the Fall. His all-seeing eyes had failed him. Ashâke shuddered.

"Our crafty brother," said a voice behind her.

She started, whipped around to find Arewa leaning casually against the doorpost, gourd at hand. "Arewa," she gasped. Ashâke wondered if he had been watching her while she slept. She wouldn't put it past him. Once, he had waded into the river with her while she took a bath, and began to scrub her back, completely unabashed and heedless to her protests.

She felt for the other orisha and took their locations, scattered about the caravansary.

"How long have you been standing there?"

The god simply smiled at her as he swaggered into the room. He wandered over to Eshu's statue and touched a hand to his face. "Do you know how he lost his eyes?" he asked.

"Didn't he . . . play a cruel trick on the Supreme Father . . . ?" asked Ashâke, rifling through her memory of her lessons in the temple.

"Yes. I don't think I'd ever seen Father that angry," muttered Arewa. "I think he wanted to kill him. I for one would have loved to see that—don't look at me like that, you don't know Eshu. No, really. You don't." He gave a dramatic sigh, turning back to the statue. "Instead, Father took his eyes and sewed shut his lips. You know . . . I've always wondered what he did to make Father so angry. He never said. And neither did Eshu, for that matter—even though I pressed him." Arewa gulped from his gourd, wiped his mouth on the back of his hand. "He seemed to have learned his lesson. No more space to grow another mouth," he mused, then tapped at the statue's neck. "Although I suppose he could have grown one here, though that would make him rather hideous to look at, don't you think?"

"Er . . ."

"Rather hideous indeed. And *un*-pretty. Unlike me." He preened. Arewa sank onto the mat, folding his legs beneath him. He chugged from his gourd, throat stone bobbing and bobbing. Then he belched, and began to laugh. "I remember when he played one of his tricks on Koriko. She was so incensed that she trapped him in a tree."

Ashâke frowned. "In a tree?"

"An iroko tree. Held him there for . . . a hundred seasons?"

"Eighty-nine," said Ogun, who had quietly slipped into the room. "I counted. And it wasn't long enough."

Ashâke found herself intrigued. It was rare that the gods spoke of their past lives. "Couldn't he . . . free himself?"

"Oh. Oh ho ho ho." Arewa wagged a finger at her,

shaking his head. "Trees are old, older than us all. Even Koriko, being goddess of all trees and vegetation, had a tough time bending them to her will. Anyway, she trapped Eshu for . . . eighty-nine seasons—"

"Not long enough," said Ogun.

"—and it wasn't until everything started to fall apart that she released him."

"What do you mean, 'everything started to fall apart'?" asked Ashâke.

"He couldn't fulfil his duties anymore, on account of being trapped in the tree and all. So people started dying. Without Eshu there to control them, the roads began to . . . come undone. You could set out from your village to another village, a perfectly straight path, and end up lost in the desert, or the jungle. Mortals cried and petitioned. Eshu's priests spent their lives praying to him, but of course he couldn't respond."

"Because of the—"

He gestured wildly. "Take this place for example. The forest is all gone."

"The forest?"

"Aha. This desert you see used to be lush greenery, filled with all kinds of fruit. Fruits you can only dream of. And wondrous animals. Wood elves and egbere and spectral birds with wings of light—a forest alive with pure ashe. Very much like Orun. But Koriko is—" He broke off, a storm in his brows.

99

Ashâke peered out the window at the desert, at the hard, red earth and silver moon, at the jagged mountains whipped by dry eastern winds, and she tried to picture it covered in verdant vegetation. Roots filling the cracks in the earth and tall trees offering shade.

"What will happen if . . ."

She could not bring herself to say it, but Arewa said it for her. "If we all die?"

"The world will perish," said Oya, joining them.

Ashâke looked at her in alarm. "What?"

"Ashe," said the goddess, "is the divine energy that animates every thing in the world. The very substance from which Olodumare formed the world from nothing. We orisha are mere custodians of various aspects of creation."

Ashâke knew all this, she had been instructed in the temple. The orisha were Olodumare's children, but they were also his many aspects, various pieces of himself he'd broken off to lord over parts of creation. But she had never thought . . . it never even *occurred* to her to consider such an outcome, that without them . . .

"Seal off a room," Oya continued, "and the torches will still burn . . . until they don't. In the same manner, if we were all to perish the skies would still bring rain, the seas would still bring wind. But only for a while, because they remember. Without us, without our guidance . . . eventually . . ." She trailed off, the weight of the unspoken words heavy in the air.

Ashâke found herself thoroughly shaken by this revelation.

"It is already happening," said Yemoja. "And now, with their brazen attack, turning mortals against us, it is happening faster. We are here for a reason. That is one thing the godkillers don't think of. If we die, the world dies."

SEVEN

The snake-wine burned as it went down Djábri's throat, but he welcomed the burn. It made him alert, not that he needed to be any more alert, his inability to sleep having brought him here in the first place.

The inn was nearly empty. But that wasn't unusual for such late hours. Several patrons lay passed out across the tables. In the corner a troupe of mummers, still garbed in garish make-up and attire from their play, engaged in a very sleepy game of ayò. Behind the bar the innkeep swayed in a cloud of smoke, sucking ponderously on a floute. A blind singer was perched next to the bar, offering a half-hearted rendition of "Moremi My Love." Half-hearted on account of him being asleep most of the time; every now and then he would jerk awake to deliver a line, fingers fumbling at his kora strings, before relapsing into stupor. His empty collection cup lay at his feet, having been relieved of its coins moments earlier by an exiting patron.

Altogether it was a sorry establishment, but it suited Djábri just fine. He did not frequent such inns, but mind churning, he had wanted a place to consider his thoughts, someplace he wouldn't be easily recognised. Which wasn't easy, considering he was captain of the Ogboni and all.

Djábri took another gulp of snake-wine. He reached into his pocket and produced the rock, turning it over in his hand. He called it a rock, but that was because he had no idea what to call it. Some kind of gemstone? A piece of metal? It was dull grey. But it did not always remain that colour. It had been sea blue, then emerald green, then the purple of twilight. It seemed every time he brought the rock out it changed into a different colour. It was a remarkable thing, quite unlike anything he had ever seen, and Djábri could not deny the fact that he was quite taken with it. It had slipped from the Guardian's pouch as he hauled her to the cells in the flood tunnels, and he had grabbed it without thought. He was not a thief. He had been trying to get her to safety before someone came along—Yaruddin had missed them by mere seconds—and he had forgotten all about it. It wasn't until he flung his exhausted self into bed that he felt it in his pocket.

Djábri found that if he stared at the rock too long he felt . . . brave. The world seemed brighter, his thoughts clearer, and for an hour or two afterwards he went about with immense clarity and surety of mind. It was special, there was no doubt about that, and the Guardian must have had it on her person for a reason. So he found himself looking at it every opportunity he got, thinking of a way to save his brother. But for the life of him he couldn't figure out what it was. He found himself reaching for it at every turn, idly rubbing his hand over it. He thought it would have been worn smooth with his constant fiddling, but it wasn't. He would return it. He had wanted to return it, but it was precious to him . . .

"A fine piece o' rock."

The singer slipped into place at his table. He wore a dirty purple hat, and up close Djábri could make out long scars on his arms, as though he had been clawed by a leopard. But that wasn't what set Djábri's spine tingling: it was the fact that he wore a grin that was a little too friendly. It was the fact that he looked suddenly a little too alert, as though he hadn't spent half the night snoozing. It was the fact that he had commented on the piece.

"You see it?" asked Djábri.

"Yes."

Djábri looked at the worn strip of rag wrapped around the singer's eyes. "Aren't you blind?"

The man smiled, and Djábri realised that there were several holes in his lips. "These eyes do not work. But I have not lost my sight. I see much more than you can imagine. I know, for example, of the rascal who relieved me of my coins when he thought I was snoozing. It will please you to know that he was robbed of those very same coins and beaten to within an inch of his life. Poetic justice, eh?"

Djábri frowned. He honestly did not know what to make of this. Was he a swindler, then, pretending to be blind? That had to be it. Behind that rag his eyes were whole. Perhaps his associates had jumped that unfortunate fellow and beaten him to near death. Either way Djábri was not in the mood. He turned away from him and downed another cup of snake-wine.

The man leant his kora against the table and settled into his chair. "So. Where did you find it?"

"That's none of your business," snapped Djábri, slipping the rock into his pocket. "And I'll thank you to leave me alone."

The stranger remained unfazed. "I think, you'll find, that it is my business. I know because it doesn't belong to you."

A chill went through Djábri. Swift and surreptitious, he scanned the dark room. The mummers were still at their game; the innkeep was now wiping down some cups with a greasy cloth. Djábri glanced out the dusty windows and was confronted with a patina of darkness. Finally he looked at the stranger. "Who are you?"

"Ah . . ." The stranger broke into a disturbing smile. "Now you're asking questions. But you ask the *wrong* question."

Djábri squinted at the man. It seemed his features were constantly shifting. Sometimes he looked like an old man, his face lined with wrinkles; other times he looked younger than Djábri, boyish face spry with youth. He looked vaguely, disturbingly familiar, although Djábri could not quite place his finger on it. Djábri frowned at the jug, wondering if the snake-wine was addling his mind.

"Fuck it," he growled, pushing to his feet. Whatever this was, he had no time for it. He started to turn away—

The stranger's hand shot out and closed around Djábri's wrist in a vise grip.

"Please," he said. "Don't walk away from me. That would be rude."

"If by the time I count to five," Djábri growled, "you haven't removed your hand, you will lose it. Permanently."

The inn grew quiet. Djábri was vaguely aware that the mummers had stopped playing, and had turned to watch the scene; the innkeep was looking at them, an expression of concern on his face. The stranger still held his hand in a bony clasp, and for a moment Djábri thought—*hoped*—he wouldn't let go. For a moment, he saw himself whipping out his cleaver. A single slash and his hand would thud to the floor. But then the moment passed, and the man's hand fell away, and Djábri was turning to leave, disappointed.

He stepped out into the night.

A gust of wind blew into his face as he started down the street and he gathered his cloak about him. With one hand he felt for the reassuring bulge of the rock in his pocket. Blood still roared in his ears, and his heart still thrashed in his chest. He had been spoiling for a fight. All this pent-up anger, all this pent-up rage, with no release.

It started to rain. The rain came down in sheets, drummed on roofs, and turned the streets into rapids. Djábri hunched over against the deluge and cut to the right, taking the route that went through the market. The shops and stalls were grotesque shapes in the dark. With a shriek the wind tore the flimsy roof off one of the shacks and sent it spinning into the night.

Someone was blocking his path.

Djábri stopped some ten paces from the figure. What were the odds that this was just some pedestrian? But would a simple pedestrian be blocking his path at such a late hour, not sheltering from the rain? Not to mention, the man was standing at a market crossroads at the darkest hour of night, and he could hear his ma's voice, telling him it was an omen. Djábri reached for his cleaver.

"You cannot run from me."

The voice came at him from all sides, as though he were at the bottom of a well and there was nothing but echoes, eerie susurrations of a ghostly voice, or two, or three.

"You cannot run from me."

Clouds shifted from the face of the moon, turning night to day, and in the brief moment of illumination he saw it was the singer, that same sick smile plastered on his face.

"You—" Djábri began. *How did he get here so fast?* Djábri had left the man at the inn and there was only one road that led to the market and he had taken it. He blinked rainwater from his eyes, and when he looked again the man was gone. "What the—?" He wheeled about, slowly scanning the dark. "Show yourself! I'm not playing games. Whoever you are, I swear—"

Laughter. A baritone guffaw. It came at Djábri from all sides and sent a current of terror sliding down his spine. Djábri wheeled wildly to the right, brandishing his cleaver, and found the stranger seated on an upturned clay pot, wrinkled face slick with rain. But he was not alone. Perched high on the roof was the same man, wearing that rictus of a grin. Twins? Then he saw them, spread about the market like tentpoles. There were ten, fifteen, twenty of them, all of them the same man in the purple hat and dirty traveller's clothing.

Djábri shook his head. He was losing his mind.

He charged, slashed at the one nearest to him. But his blade cut through air, and the man was at his ear, whispering everything he did not want to hear.

"*You've told yourself it isn't your fault, but it is, it is.*"

"*It is,*" the other one echoed.

"Shut up!" Djábri screamed. "Shut up and face me!"

It seemed to him the darkness had thickened, as though someone had thrown a blanket over the moon. Djábri strained, struggling to see, the rain beating at him, the wind whipping at him. He did not like this. He did not like this one bit. His soldier instincts told him to take cover, to seek refuge until he could assess the situation. But he could not see. Good gods, *he could not see.* So he spun about, slashing as the voices taunted him from every side.

"Tell us the truth."

He buried his cleaver into the chest of one of them. "Oops." The stranger grinned before dissolving into black sand.

"What do you want with me?"

One of them appeared at his right, his breath hot in Djábri's ear. *"Tell the truth."*

Another at his left. *"Tell."*

"Tell yourself *the truth."*

"What truth?" screamed Djábri. "What bloody truth?"

"Tell us about Djola . . . DJOLAAAAA."

"No!" yelled Djábri, slashing wildly, slashing at nothing. "No. Shut up! Shut your fucking—!"

Something tugged at his feet and Djábri saw in horror that he was sinking. Sinking into a ground that had turned to quicksand. He panicked and jerked his leg but the mud only pulled harder, faster. It was up to his knees now. A raw, animal panic overcame him. His cleaver flew out of his grip and vanished into the mud. Then they were pouring out of the shops, more copies of that man who Djábri now knew was no man, was no ordinary man, spilling out of the ground as if from the bowels of Apadi itself. They gathered around him, wearing identical grins.

"Tell us," they chanted. "Tell us."

Through the fog of panic and confusion and terror, a thought came to Djábri with clarity: he was going to die. He was going to die hounded by a spirit in the middle of the market. He was going to die buried beneath roiling mud. He thought of his ma, who had lost one son already. Losing him too would break her, he knew that. And what about Ralia? Who would protect her from the Ogboni? From the godkillers? And . . . and Djola. *Who would save Djola?*

He burst into tears. "Djola."

"Yesss."

"I'm sorry." Snot and spit dribbled down his chin. "I'm so sorry . . . Djola . . ."

And then, the truth came tumbling from his lips.

All his life he had dreamed of making it into the palace guard. And he had toiled day and night to achieve that dream. He had felt so much pride when the old captain told him he had made it into the distinguished ranks of the Oba's palace guard. Granted, his position lifted his family from the dregs of poverty, but it was pride he felt each morning as he donned his armour, as he walked into the palace, knowing that he had the most sacred duty. And he had attended his duty with such devotion and fervour that when half a season later the old captain retired, he had named Djábri his successor, and the Oba ratified the decision. Oh, the pride. The joy he had felt. And then Djola had come along, wanting to join the ranks of the palace guard, working harder than anyone else. Djábri failed him on purpose, not wanting to share the glory. There was only space for one Fadeyi in the palace. Never mind that Djola had looked up to him, never mind that Djola had followed him about, wanting to do everything his older brother did. They had argued, said some words they didn't mean, words Djábri now wished he could take back. And Djola had been so vexed he had left, left to stay with their nomad griot relatives, moving from place to place. Last Djábri heard he had been a watchman.

It was all his fault. If he hadn't pushed him away, driven him to join their relatives, he wouldn't be . . . he wouldn't be . . .

"I deserve it," he sobbed. "I deserve to die." Death would free him from this aching pain he carried in his heart, from this guilt that ate at him.

"Siblings," said the stranger, and his voice was no longer a chorus. "They drive us mad. Tug at our basest instincts, because no one knows us better. We wish death upon them. I should know. I've . . . had my fair share of sibling troubles. And we do things. But we don't really mean it. I didn't . . . really mean it. Or maybe I did. It doesn't matter. The deed is done, and as you have learned, actions have consequences."

Somewhere a dog let loose a forlorn howl.

Djabri looked up at the stranger. What was he waffling on about? But he pushed that from his mind, because he realised then that he was on his knees in the middle of the market, sobbing and blubbering like a baby. He blinked, confused. The skies were clear. The ground was dry. And most importantly, there was no quicksand.

"What in the . . ." He stumbled to his feet, wiping his eyes. He was alive. Good gods, he was alive.

The stranger was sitting on the ground next to him, twirling his cap in his hands.

"What did you do?" gasped Djábri. "Who are you?"

When the stranger looked at him he saw that he had taken off the strip of clothing that hid his eyes. He was truly blind—ruined orifices where his eyes should be and his lips . . .

His lips were sewn shut with copper wire. Djábri gaped, the truth scrabbling to the fore of his mind, baring itself before him—

"You're Eshu Elegba," breathed Djábri. "Lord of mischief . . ."

The Lord of Disease and Malady

A shadow passed over Yinka and he looked up in time to see a great bird bank low, folding its wings as it fell into a deep dive. It fell like a rock, fell fast towards the ground, and just when Yinka thought it would crash, it spread its great wings, beating up a storm so powerful he was nearly thrown off his feet. The bird landed in front of him.

It was easily the most beautiful bird Yinka had ever seen. The feathers on its head and neck were midnight black, with a crest the colour of fire. Its wing and saddle feathers were bursting with vivid colours of green and yellow and violet, all the colours of the rainbow, and then some. Colours Yinka had no name for. They seemed to shift each time Yinka looked at them. Powerful legs ended in three wicked-looking talons that dug into the earth. The bird was easily tall as three men and twice as long. It regarded Yinka through fiery eyes, snorting and snapping a long curved beak as sharp as steel. For a moment Yinka thought it would attack him, that surely this was some man-eating bird—

"So you're looking for Shopona." said the bird. "Don't look so surprised. Word travels around these parts."

"Yes," gasped Yinka once he had overcome his shock. "I am looking for him."

"I will take you to him. But you must give me something in return."

"What?" asked Yinka, apprehensive.

"Reach into your pouch, and give me the first thing your hand touches."

Yinka rooted around in his pouch and produced two sorry-looking pieces of bitter kola.

The bird seemed to consider a moment. "I'll take it."

Yinka placed the kola nuts gingerly on the ground, all the while keeping his eyes on that sharp beak. The bird pecked at both nuts before vanishing them into the darkness of her gullet. She lowered herself to the ground.

"Clamber on, mortal."

Yinka mounted the bird and seized a handful of feathers to steady himself. He felt his stomach lurch as she took to the skies, the wind whipping into his eyes as she climbed higher and higher. As they flew through the clouds Yinka chanced a glance at the world below and inhaled sharply in wonderment. Rivers of molten silver, mountains belching liquid gold. Several gargantuan structures rose from the greenery, edifices of mind-bending architecture that the bird told him were the courts of various orisha. He glimpsed the Supreme Father's court, gold and shining in the sun. They sailed over enchanted forests, forests that seemed to sing, a pleasant choral music emanating from the trees. Yinka glimpsed several groves that bore fruits that were crystals of light. He saw strange climbing trees with leaves so vast they could hold half a dozen elephants. The leaves reached out as if to snatch them from the sky and the bird climbed higher.

Yinka wished his daughter were here to see it all. To witness the beauty and wonder of the domain of the gods. People who had gone to Conclaves often said that there were no words in all the languages of the world to describe Orun, and as he clung on to the bird, watching the Seat of the Orisha unravel beneath him, Yinka found that they were right.

"What are those?"

"Prayers," she said. "Petitions, sacrifices."

So this was where his prayers were going, unattended. "There are . . . so many of them," said Yinka. But of course, there would be. How many people, at any given time, were afflicted with one ailment or the other? So why hadn't Shopona attended to them? He voiced the question.

"He's been . . . busy," said the bird. "They've all been busy."

"Busy?"

"You'll see."

With a screech the bird stretched her great wings and launched into the sky.

The court of Shopona was a vast, roofless chamber that opened to the sky. The lord of disease and maladies presented a grisly sight. His skin was a sickly-green hue and covered in suppurating sores. Flies buzzed around his head. He sat in his throne, specks of spit dribbling into his beard as he chomped on fruits. Even as Yinka watched, he took a swig from his chalice, then belched. A great swarm of locusts sprung from his mouth, fluttered high into the sky, and vanished into clouds. Hundreds upon hundreds of orisha were gathered in the chamber, seated as they watched with rapt attention the scene in the centre.

A great white serpent was coiled around a short and stocky orisha with a floor-length beard and hair on his back who Yinka recognised as Anjonu, lord of trolls, stone-men, and other such denizens of the deep forest. The beast opened its jaws wide to swallow the god, but then stopped, massive head cocked towards Anjonu. It seemed to listen for a moment or two, then released the god, uncoiling its great length.

"You cheated!" roared Shopona, leaping to his feet. "The rules were no powers. You fight as mortals!"

"I did," said Anjonu. "Mortals have no power, so they must navigate life with nothing but their wit, as I just did."

"Wit, you say?" called Arewa as he poured himself a drink. "Huh. Consider me flabbergasted."

The arena erupted in laughter. Anjonu swivelled his thick neck, brow clouding as he regarded the crowd. Then he turned back to Arewa. "Do you mock me?"

"Oh, I would neeeever do that. I have no wish to come under the ire of your blistering wit."

Anjonu considered a moment. "No. I think you mock me."

"Enough! Enough!" roared Shopona, pounding the arm of his throne. "Anjonu. What did you tell the beast to make it release you?"

"I told it, 'Release me or I'll turn you into a troll.'"

"Ah," said Arewa. "Well *that* explains it."

More thunderous laughter. A god next to Yinka slid out of his chair, snorting and grunting with mirth.

"Next challenge!" called the lord of disease and maladies, waving Anjonu away.

Yinka watched the gods guffaw, his ears growing slowly hot. This was what had them, had Shopona, occupied and unable to attend to prayers? *This?*

"SHOPONA!" he cried, striding into the centre of the court. "SHOPONAAAAA!!!"

The court fell silent.

"A mortal," someone said. "Is this part of the game?"

Shopona blinked. He leaned into Yemoja and said in a theatrical whisper, "Is there a Conclave I'm unaware of?"

"No. It isn't for another moon."

"Then who let this mortal in?"

"That would be Eshu. Saddle him with one task and he can't even do that properly."

"Perhaps Father should take out his new eyes," said Arewa.

"Oh, he'll just grow another pair." And they dissolved into tinkling laughter.

Yinka could not believe it. They were . . . they were like children. "My daughter is ill!" Yinka yelled, each word tearing out of his throat. "My daughter has been ill for three moons. We've offered sacrifices, done everything possible to appease you. I brought my very best hide as a gift." Yinka looked around. "Will none of you help me? Please."

"Oh just—answer him and let us continue," said Oya.

Shopona glared at Oya. "I don't tell you how to conduct your affairs, do I? I do not take orders from a mortal. I am not beholden to them, nor to you." He turned to Yinka. "Leave my sight before I smite you with disease."

"But my daughter . . ."

Shopona closed his eyes, opened them. "Dead. She's dead. Now get out!"

Yinka's mouth went dry. "W-what?" he croaked into the silence.

"Is he deaf or something?" Shopona wondered aloud.

Yinka's knees buckled. He staggered backwards even as his vision turned watery. "No," he said, shaking his head.

"No," he repeated, as if invoking that one word would make it untrue. "She can't be. You must be mistaken."

Shopona's eyebrow went up. "*I* must be mistaken? She's been dead half a moon."

Half a moon. That was . . . that was when he set out. Enitan must have died shortly after he left. Yinka collapsed to the floor, and let loose a howl of anguish. Enitan was dead. *Dead*. Had she called for him in her last moments and he hadn't been there? Had she . . . had she suffered? He had dawdled too long. If only he had come here earlier, if only . . .

Shopona looked perplexed. "Is he crying?" He chuckled uneasily. "I hate it when they do that. You. Human. Stop it."

"You could have helped her," Yinka wept. "You could have saved her!"

Shopona frowned. "Maybe. But I don't trade in hypotheticals. Your daughter's dead, so what? Go breed. You'll have another—"

"BUT SHE WAS A CHILD!" Yinka screamed. "A CHILD! *What petty, heartless god would bring disease on a child?*"

A terrible hush blanketed the court.

Yinka stumbled to his feet, looking around at the shocked faces of the orisha. Some small part of him told him to stop, but he had run mad from grief. "Look at you. Look at you all." He laughed, a long, mad sound in the hall.

"Mighty, mighty orisha who can't be bothered to attend your duties. My daughter was ill. For three moons I offered sacrifices. Did everything to appease you, so you could heal her. But my prayers went unattended, unheard, because you were too busy *playing games*. You were all too occupied with your games. I revered you. I worshipped you. But you are like children. Petty, oversized children with immense power and little regard for our lives—"

Shopona sprang suddenly to his feet, sending the fruit-laden tray crashing to the floor. He stretched out an arm. Yinka felt a tugging around his midriff, and then he was flying, yanked through the air by some invisible cord towards Shopona. The orisha caught him by the throat and held him up for all to see, dangling him by his neck some sixty feet from the floor. The orisha brought Yinka so close to his face he could see the vertical snake-slits of his eyes, the foul sores on his face. Shopona's lips peeled back as he growled, "I could curse you with maladies that would make you wish you had never been born. I could make it so you'd never die. You would beg for death, and I would bring you to its cusp, only to heal you, and invent fresh maladies to torture you. But stretching out your death would mean you were worth my attention—" Then he began to choke Yinka.

Instincts kicked into action. Yinka struggled, beating against Shopona's arm, but he might as well have been beating at a tree trunk. The orisha held him in a death grip, slowly crushing his neck. Yinka felt his legs kick and spasm, his body, his mind struggling to save itself. But Yinka did not want to save himself. What use was a life without his daughter? It was better he died, and spare himself a lifetime of misery and pain.

"O mighty . . . mighty god," Yinka mocked, spittle flying from his lips. "O valiant, petty god. Kill me—"

A burst of mirthless laughter gargled up his lips, and he laughed even harder when he glimpsed Shopona's furious, confused expression. A haze of red burst into his vision, something sticky and hot running down his cheeks, and it wasn't until he tasted blood that he realised his eyes were bleeding.

A loud pop went off in Yinka's left ear—and then nothing. He could hear nothing in that ear! And then darkness seeped into the corner of his vision, and he closed his eyes, welcoming death—

The pressure vanished from his neck. Yinka opened his eyes just in time to see Shopona fling him away with a look of disgust. Yinka sailed through the air, and then he was on the floor, tumbling and bouncing. Burning lines opened across his elbows and knees, but he barely registered them, as he lay there on the floor gasping.

He pushed to all fours, heaving like a donkey.

Shopona descended the stairs to his throne. He strode towards Yinka, then squatted before him. "Mortals," he said softly. "How precious and all-encompassing your lives and woes may seem. But what you must understand is that from my perspective, your existence is merely a blip. I blink, and a thousand seasons have passed. Why, I can barely remember the names of the priests who carry my favour for that matter. Tomorrow I will not remember you." He cupped Yinka's chin, forcing him to look up at him. "You, on the other hand . . . you will spend your days seething with rage, but ultimately helpless, as all mortals are, to do anything about it." He made shooing motions with his hands. "Now, go. You've interrupted my game long enough. And be grateful I do not smite you for your insolence." He straightened, offered Yinka an empty smile, and then turned and strode for his seat.

EIGHT

Djábri hated dungeons. He hated the cold, dark oppressiveness of them. He hated the lightless cells, and the dank walls that always seemed to inch closer. They reminded him too much of the mines in Abeokuta where he had worked as a youth, before they caved in. Later they told him he had been trapped underground for nearly three days, but those three days had felt like seasons. Time had lost all meaning in the dark places beneath the earth, with the weight and stench of his dead elephant on him. Each elephant was paired to a rider, who hitched ore-laden wagons to harnesses and dragged them out of the mines. He had thought he would die. He joined the Oba's guard shortly after that, avoiding dungeons and small places whenever he could.

Djábri stared at the stairs that descended into the palace dungeons, wishing he were anywhere but here. It had taken all of his willpower to go into the tunnels where he'd hidden the Guardian. Ashâke. She'd said her name was Ashâke. He hoped she made it safely to Abeokuta.

Eshu was out there roaming. Djábri had thought all the remaining orisha were with Ashâke—or *in* her? He never understood it all. This matter of gods and godkillers and idan. It all went over his head. And now, many days later, it seemed a fever dream, a hallucination brought on by heavy drinking. He had returned to the inn, to be sure, and queried the innkeep, who insisted the blind singer had not followed Djábri, but remained in the inn until the small hours of morning. So Djábri was forced to chalk it all up to his guilt. All he did was for Djola. He took a deep breath to still himself and went into the dungeons.

Moans welcomed him. Forlorn groans from wretched souls—people he and his men had rounded up—laced the air. In the beginning the dungeons had been brimming with prisoners: adepts, priests and priestesses, common folk who'd refused to renounce the orisha. Now there was just the lone prisoner or two, gaunt arms scrabbling between bars as he walked past, begging for a drop of water, cursing him, raving weakly. Djábri shook off their arms and marched deeper into the dungeon. Spending so long in the dark, without light or human contact. It did things to the mind. Stars above, how he hated this place. How he hated himself.

Djábri reached into his pocket, shuddering with audible relief as he closed his hand around the rough rock. The effect was instantaneous: his unease, his fear, melted away so that when he finally found the cell he was looking for, he had assumed his usual blank expression.

The cell door was ajar and Djábri stepped in to find Yaruddin staring into the corner. He didn't turn at Djábri's approach. A modicum of unease stole into Djábri's heart. Had he just been . . . standing in the dark? What a freak. What a terrible, terrible freak.

Djábri cleared his throat. "You called for me, my lord?"

Yaruddin grunted absent-mindedly. He gestured with a ringed pinky. "You know this woman, yes?"

Djábri glanced at the corner, where he made out a wretched figure. So that was what Yaruddin had been staring at. The woman stirred feebly under Djábri's gaze. Horrible burns adorned her arms and neck, and there was an ungodly stench wafting from her direction. He lifted his torch and she shied away from the light, cowering like an abused animal. But there was enough light for him to see her swollen face, her broken nose that had not been set. With a jolt Djábri realised he knew her. A priestess of Yemoja who'd publicly denounced her orisha when the godkillers first took the city, wife to Chief Ajanlekoko, one of the noble chiefs who had served under Oba Badamosi before Yaruddin drowned him and took his throne.

"Simbi," Djábri croaked.

"What?"

"Her name is Simbi, my lord. Simbi Ajanlekoko."

There came the sound of footfalls and the ring of shackles and Djábri turned to see Leaf leading a prisoner towards them. Chief Ajanlekoko. When last Djábri had seen him he had been robust, wearing his potbelly with pride—a sign of his status. Now his filthy clothes hung off his frail form like an old sailcloth. Haunted eyes peered out of sunken sockets. Leaf pushed the man into the cell and dumped him next to his wife.

"My lord," he said, struggling to his knees. "I don't understand. My wife—"

"She failed me," said Yaruddin. "She had the Guardian in her grasp, in your house, and she let her go."

"No," Simbi rasped, struggling to her knees. "I didn't let her go. I did all you asked, I swear! I sent word the moment I saw her—"

"The very moment?"

A pause. Simbi's eyes darted in desperation from Yaruddin to Djábri to Leaf. "She was wary. I needed—I needed to make her believe me!"

Ajanlekoko licked his lips. "Give me a chance. Give us another chance. She won't fail you." He turned to Simbi. "Isn't that so?"

Simbi nodded so hard it looked like her head would fall off.

"It's too late for all that. The Guardian is in the wind, and won't return to Inysha. You have lost the element of surprise." Yaruddin stretched his hand to his side and a black mist appeared, slowly condensing to form that terrible scimitar. He took a step towards them. Simbi scrambled behind her husband, lips trembling.

"Please!" Simbi wailed, fat tears falling down her cheeks. "Please—my children—"

Yaruddin paused, then said to Leaf, "Release him."

Leaf fumbled for a key, then unshackled the chief. Ajanlekoko rubbed his wrists, scraping and bowing. "Thank you. Thank you, my lord. You're too kind—"

"Yes." Yaruddin's voice was soft, expressionless. "The Teacher teaches us to temper justice with mercy. But there will be justice." He handed his scimitar by the hilt to Ajanlekoko. "Kill her."

Djábri's heart lurched. Simbi's eyes widened in terror. Ajanlekoko's face spasmed in confusion. "My—my lord?" croaked the chief.

"Please," she gasped. She caught Djábri's eyes. "Please. I'm just like you. I'm—"

Tears leaked down her ruined face. Djábri avoided her eyes, but he could not shut out her sobs, which needled at him, needled at his conscience. "Please. I have children. Little boys! They're friends with Ralia—"

He met her eyes, saw the absolute dejection in them. He had long learned to detach, to numb himself to the atrocities he committed in a bid to save his brother. But if Djola were to see him right now, would he be appalled? Would he be ashamed? Djábri already knew what his ma thought of him. He had tried to rationalise, to explain that all he did was for Djola. But now he was not so sure the cost fit the price. Granted, he hadn't yet taken a life. But he had rounded up his people, thrown them in dungeons. He had stood by as the godkillers made examples of them. He *was* already complicit. He was a monster.

What sort of a monster would he be if he simply stood by, if he let this woman die here tonight? What manner of monster would watch a man murder his wife? A woman who, through no fault of hers, had only been trying to survive as best she could. It would break the man, and break the children. And he knew already all too well what it was to live with guilt. His soul was already damned, he knew that. Djábri closed his eyes, and inhaled slowly.

Simbi's wretched sobs pierced like a needle, weighed like an anchor on his conscience. He couldn't do it. It was all too much.

Djábri's eyes snapped open. In one fluid movement he chopped the blade out of Ajanlekoko's hand. It clattered to the floor and he scooped it up, pinning Yaruddin to the wall. He pressed the blade to Yaruddin's throat. Blood roared in his ears. Everything was happening so fast, and there was no time to think, no time to second-guess himself. He wished he could touch the rock now, to clear his mind.

"Captain?" asked Leaf.

"Stay back!" Djábri yelled. Leaf was a coward, but he

was a self-preserving coward who would want to remain in Yaruddin's good graces. So Djábri kept him in his line of sight.

"Djábri." Yaruddin looked unbothered, as though this was all a slight annoyance. "What do you think you're doing?"

"Release him," Djábri growled, spittle flying from his lips. He pressed the scimitar harder and a bead of blood appeared beneath the steel, quickly calcifying.

"Of course. All he need do is kill his wife."

"Release *my brother*. Take me instead!"

"Your brother?" For a moment, confusion curdled Yaruddin's features, then understanding flashed in his eyes. He began to laugh. A full-bellied laugh that echoed through the dungeons. "You know, Djábri, I wondered. I always wondered about you. The way you stuck close, the zeal with which you carried out your duties. Some fool would have taken it as proof of your devotion, of your love for the Teacher. But I am old, and I knew there was something about you." He stopped laughing, but the mirth remained in his eyes. "So this body belongs to your brother, eh?"

"Yes. And you *will* release him. Djola! Can you hear me? I know you're in there! Fight him! Fight him, brother!"

"He's gone, fool! He's dead. And there is nothing of him that exists. Oh ho ho ho. Is this your grand plan, then? To stay close to me? To free your brother?" Yaruddin guffawed.

"Let me tell you what happens when I Eat mortals. I take your memories, your fears and aspirations. I take all that you are, all that you could be, and make it mine. I become you. But sometimes I simply let it all go and assume your skin. Perhaps I shouldn't have in this case. I would have realised who you were—"

"No," said Djábri, tears stinging his eyes. He blinked furiously. "You're lying. Djola!"

"Am I? Let me show you."

Pain exploded behind his eyes. Djábri cried out, staggering backwards. He struck at his brow as if to wrench away the pain, as if to claw out his eyeballs. He tumbled over something and crashed to the floor. He opened his eyes and through the haze of pain and panic he saw Yaruddin slumped against the wall, lifeless. And with a pang of fresh terror he understood that whatever animated his brother's body was no longer there. It was in him.

Yaruddin was trying to Eat him.

"No!" he gasped. "Get out of my—"

He had wanted this. His body, his soul in exchange for his brother's, but not if it was all futile, not if Djola no longer existed. Djábri felt a strange dark presence in his mind, stretching, forcing its way in. He fought, a mangled cry of fury and fear escaping his throat as he tried to flee from that dark swarm. But it was like running underwater, it was like running backwards, and the thing rapidly closed the gap between—

Djábri's grasping hands closed around something rough and small. At first he thought it a loose piece of flagstone, but then a familiar heat flared through his body, clarity flooded his mind, and his fears fell away.

A violent spasm rocked his body, and he felt an *expulsion,* as though he were throwing up. A long, bloodcurdling scream pierced the air and when he opened his eyes he saw Djola's body had come alive, animated, and it was kicking and frothing at the mouth. The eyes flew open, then rolled in their sockets until Djábri could only see the whites of them. Whites that burst and began to leak blood.

He heard screams. His own screams. But also Leaf yelling, "Captain! Captain!"

He dropped to his knees, crawling. He could scarcely see.

Djábri sat there for one long moment, stupefied, heart beating frantically in his chest. Then he looked down to find himself clutching the rock. It was glowing a fiery orange, like a small sun in his hand. It must have rolled out of his pocket when he collapsed. Somehow the rock had saved him.

Yaruddin had grown utterly still.

"Captain?" asked Leaf, uncertain. "Is he . . . dead?"

"I don't know."

He didn't know if they could die. The one thing he knew was that Yaruddin had tried to Eat him and failed. The rock had saved him.

He had to leave. He had to flee this place before the others came. And there were others in the palace. Heart thudding in his ears, he pushed to his feet.

"We have to go!" he yelled. "Now. GO! GO!"

Simbi and Ajanlekoko scrambled to their feet and Djábri pounded down the corridor, out of the dungeon, and into the night.

NINE

Yar was aware of a tangy metallic taste in his mouth. A flurry of twitches spasmed up his face as he wiped the crusted blood from his cheeks. He made out vague shapes in the dark cell—filthy rags that made for blankets, the upturned pail and slush of excrement—but none of them were the Ajanlekokos. They had escaped, no doubt aided by Leaf and Djábri . . .

Yar shuddered. Of all the emotions that coursed through him, there was one that stood out, one he hadn't felt in a long time: fear.

His blade was gone. Fresh fury washed over him. He would find Djábri and . . . and do what? Ever since the Teacher made him immortal he had not faced a foe he could not defeat. Not even the orisha. Until now. He had been repelled by Djábri's talisman. Yar had thought himself invincible, but he had come very close to being unmade. If he had tried any harder to Eat Djábri . . .

Now he found himself with a newfound appreciation of his mortality.

This changed things. This changed everything.

Light footfalls. The orange glow of a torch washed across the walls, stretching the shadow of the approaching person, and a moment later a young girl of no more than thirteen seasons appeared. Sadiya, one of the followers. She gave him a quizzical look. Yar imagined the scene from her point of view: him slumped against the wall of an empty cell, buried in night soil, eyes bleeding, body ruined. A cell that had held his most prised prisoner. Shame washed over him. But before he could open his mouth to explain that he'd been bested by a mere mortal—albeit a mortal aided by some magical talisman—before he could order the followers to find them before they escaped the city, Sadiya said, "Bahl'ul is here."

Yar's heart lurched. "The Teacher?" he croaked. "Are you certain?"

But he needn't have asked. The followers were all bound together and could almost always tell each other's exact location, but were also bound to the Teacher, and where his beacon had been weak and nigh imperceptible, now it burned as bright as the sun.

"Vashek is with him."

"I see." Yar stumbled to his feet, wobbled dangerously for a moment. Sadiya rushed to steady him but he pushed her away so violently she sprawled onto her ass. "We don't want to keep them waiting."

There were more followers in the courtyard. No doubt like Sadiya, like Yar, they had all felt the Teacher's nearness and swarmed towards him, moths to a flame. They parted for him, and Yar felt their eyes as he walked past. He kept his head high and hid his limp, but he could not hide the wounds on his skin nor mask the shit stains on his clothes. The stink of night soil and defeat. Yar's eyes found Vashek first, saw that bald pate and those disapproving brows. Then he shifted his gaze to the figure to Vashek's right: the Teacher, come at last after nearly four hundred seasons.

He was garbed in a simple grey cloak, his golden braids swept up in a knot at the back of his head. He bore in one hand an intricately carved staff, one he hadn't been carrying when last Yar saw him. And he gazed steadily at Yar as he approached. In the lead-up to the Fall the Teacher had stayed with them, taught them the secrets of the world. Their goal had been simple: to free man from the yoke of the orisha. Bahl'ul had gathered the followers, malcontents like Yar who'd suffered the tyranny of the orisha, who'd sought an outlet for their pain. Yar had laughed at first when Bahl'ul told him of his plans, but when Bahl'ul showed him all that he was, all that he could do, he had been grateful to join him. He had felt a part of something bigger, more important, than himself. He had been honoured to have been chosen. But all that changed after the Fall. The Teacher vanished, and no one could say where he went, not even Vashek, who he left in charge.

"Teacher," said Yar, bowing deeply. "I am your humble servant."

"Are you indeed, Yaruddin?" said Bahl'ul.

Yar looked up. "My lord?"

"Why have you disobeyed my order?"

Yar looked from Bahl'ul to Vashek, whose lips were pressed into a grim line. "I don't understand. Your order was to destroy the orisha."

"I taught you discretion. I taught you shadow-work and self-control. But you've discarded my teachings, seeking your own glory—"

"My own glory?" said Yar, wounded. "Teacher. It has never been about glory for me. I don't know what lies Vashek—"

"Vashek carried out my wishes," said Bahl'ul, his golden eyes burning with fury. "*You,* on the other hand—"

"It's been four hundred seasons!" Yar cried. "You—you *abandoned* us! For seasons we hid in the shadows like rats, like *cowards,* when we are much, much more! People cursed us, called us godkillers, but they never knew that we did it all to liberate them! So what if I brought us out from the shadows? What if I made our presence, our goal, known? I simply took initiative. Our shadow-work proved fruitless. And you were not here to lead us." Yar fell silent, grinding his teeth. He had not given much thought to the Teacher's return, but he had imagined he would be pleased to see the work Yar had done. "Don't you see, Teacher? All I've ever done is for you. To kill the orisha. To end belief in them."

Somewhere in the night a wolf called.

"You have killed in my name," said Bahl'ul. "Visited a reign of terror on simple mortals, when our fight has not been, has never been, with mortals—"

"This is war! Has there ever been war waged without casualties? These mortals would not renounce the orisha. They were protecting them! I only did what needed be done." Blast it, why wouldn't he see reason? Why was he so concerned with trivial matters? "All this talk of hiding, of working from the shadows . . . as if they did not already know who we were. You go on about mortals—*precious mortals*—as if many did not perish in the Fall. Forgive me, but I find it all too hypocritical."

An audible gasp rang through the yard, but Yar did not care. He had had a great deal of time to think on this matter, and every one of his thoughts and grievances was coming to the fore.

"You might have started this," he blustered on, "but if we're being honest . . . this fight has been ours far longer than it's been yours. We each have a bone to pick with the orisha. And you were not here. *You were not here!* Now you—you fault me for doing what you want? What needed be done?"

Bahl'ul remained silent, watching him through burning eyes. Yar could feel the tide turn in the yard. Followers shifting, considering his words. He had been the leader, a far more effective leader than Vashek had been. Than, perhaps, even Bahl'ul. This was a case of envy, then. The Teacher had returned to find the followers doing Yar's bidding. And if Bahl'ul saw him as a rival, well, it was through no fault of his. He hadn't asked for any of this; he had simply found himself saddled with responsibility and had risen fantastically to the occasion.

"Tell me, Teacher," Yar said into the silence. "Where have you been? What have you been doing while we worked? We all thought you ran away, that you lost your stomach for our task."

Vashek cursed. He produced his scimitar and marched towards Yar, righteous fury in his eyes. Before Yar could so much as blink figures darted past him, as they formed a protective wall that stopped Vashek dead in his tracks. Yar realised then that there were two factions in the yard. On one side stood Bahl'ul and Vashek and the other followers who hadn't joined Yar's open war. On the other side stood Yar and the followers who'd pledged themselves to him. *His* followers. Each of them with scimitars drawn, ready to defend him.

Yar felt a surge of pleasure.

Vashek's lips peeled back in a snarl. "You dare question the Teacher?"

"Will the Teacher not speak for himself?" Yar took a step forwards, stretched out his arms as if to hug the world, and addressed the gathering. "Thanks to me," he bellowed, "the Guardian is on the run. She is without friend; she is without help! Thanks to me, thanks to my actions, *lord,* the orisha are greatly weakened. Few mutter prayers to them, or offer sacrifices. They are ripe for the taking!"

Once upon a time, Yar would have quailed under the Teacher's regard. Now he held his gaze, a contest of sorts, and when the Teacher looked away—bowing his head as he leaned against his staff so that it looked as though he were praying—Yar could not help but feel a surge of triumph.

"Wayward children," said Bahl'ul softly. "You have strayed far from my teachings. Still, I take full blame for what you have become. But I am here now, and I will rectify all wrongs."

"There are no wrongs to rectify. We have done well without you."

Vashek wheeled repeatedly from the Teacher to Yar, a mixture of alarm and anger on his face. "Beg," he spat as he turned once more to Yar. "Beg forgiveness. All of you. Beg the Teacher's mercy."

Beg forgiveness? Grovel? No. He would lose face before his followers.

He gave the signal and they charged.

Yar watched them blow past him, scimitars at the ready. There was no battle cry, no spirited ululations, just the silent patter of feet as they swarmed the Teacher and his group—

And then they stopped.

It seemed as though they had come up against an invisible barrier. But there they stood, frozen, two dozen flies caught in amber.

"You've grown bold in my long absence," said Bahl'ul, thunder in his eyes. "And perhaps forgotten that you all were nothing before I made you. I am the Teacher, the Great Redemptor." And he lifted his staff to the skies, lips shaping a silent word.

A great whoosh blew through the courtyard and where twenty-four followers, *Yar's* followers, had stood were pillars of fire, each one a conflagration of golden-white flames that turned night to day. Yar gaped in horror.

Their screams, high and bloodcurdling, laced with agony, filled his ears. He saw their souls, their ashe, rise, purple-black clouds of mist that were caught in those brilliant flames, until there was nothing at all where they used to be.

And then *he* was on fire. Yar couldn't tell *when* he caught on fire—one moment he had been staring in shock at his comrades and the next he was screaming himself. A terrible pain kindled in every fibre of his being and he patted at himself in a desperate bid to quench the flames, to stop that unbearable pain. But the pain he felt was not in his flesh, not in this discardable skin he wore, but in his *soul,* his very spirit, his ashe. Terror gripped him. It burned, stars above, it burned. It felt like the talisman that Djábri had used to repel him, that terrible weapon that changed things. A weapon he would have warned the Teacher and the followers about.

And now they would never know.

TEN

Four moons later, a haggard and bone-tired Ashâke glimpsed the first trees that marked the end of the desert. Abeokuta was not far off.

After leaving the caravansary, they had lost their way in the desert. Of course it had come as a shock to them, for they always headed westward, navigating by the sun's movements. They had thought themselves making good progress until Ashâke glimpsed in the distance the familiar decaying buildings of the very same caravansary they had sheltered at two moons ago.

"The roads are misbehaving," said Oya, a frown on her face.

"What roads?" rumbled Ogun, glaring through blood-shot. "It's barren earth everywhere. Blasted barren earth and blasted barren mountains and everything all looks the same!"

"Well," said Arewa, who was perched on a rock and

carefully inspecting the contents of his drinking gourd, "there's a good reason humans no longer travel the desert and the caravansaries are all abandoned."

But they had been avoiding godkillers and Ogboni, which made approaching any port to travel swiftly by sea out of the question.

"I wish for the days where with but a single thought we could spirit ourselves from one place to another. Traverse great distances!"

Ashâke, who had tuned out the orisha and was looking longingly at the caravansary, dreaming of the mouldy but soft sleeping pallets, was called back to the present when she realised the orisha had been silent awhile. She turned to find them all staring at her.

"What?" she snapped. "It's not my fault you made me idan. It's not my fault you're tied to this lowly mortal and have to move at my pace. Blame the godkillers for robbing you of your . . ." She took a deep breath and dropped to her knees, bowing deeply. "Forgive me, I meant no disrespect. I'm just exhausted . . ."

The gods were unamused. All except Arewa.

At the break of dawn, they set out again. And this time Oya took their movement by the flow of wind over the earth, by the lazy looping of scanty clouds in the sky. Now two moons later, the first smear of green interrupted the monotony of the horizon. And just beyond, looming in the distance, were the mountains of Abeokuta.

"We are close now," said Ogun, and he sniffed, large nostrils flaring. "I can smell the ores in the air."

The orisha's excitement was palpable. Ashâke felt it as a heady rush in her mind. Having traversed nearly all the kingdoms of men and found no answers, having spent so long in the desert, she had felt the weightiness of their low morale, like a heavy blanket across the face of her soul. Even Yemoja, single-minded, calculating Yemoja, had stopped plotting. They had hit a wall. But now with Abeokuta in view she felt their renewed excitement. Perhaps in Abeokuta, which had not yet fallen to godkillers, in Abeokuta, the last stronghold of man, they would find at last some answers.

"Where is it?" asked Yemoja.

"Where is what?"

"The object. The piece we found in Ile-Ife."

Ashâke licked her lips. "Em . . ."

"Have you lost your tongue?"

"I haven't seen it since Inysha."

Yemoja, for the first time, looked dumbstruck. "You— *lost* it?"

"I'm sorry—"

"Oh!" Yemoja made a strangled sound. It might have been laughter. "You're sorry!" She grabbed fistfuls of her hair as if she sought to tear them out by the roots. "The only clue we found in ten moons and you lost it! What manner of useless, witless creature are you? We never should have gone to Inysha. You think me foolish but I know you didn't lead us there to find griots or Ireti. You went there because of Simbi and she betrayed you! She betrayed you and *you lost the one useful fucking thing we found*!"

Ashâke quailed. She was back in the temple, in the Grand Hall, begging for her future as Essie yelled at her. And now, as then, it was all her fault. Tears stung her eyes. All she could think was that she was sorry. She was so, so sorry for being a terrible Guardian. She had been chosen to serve and had done a fantastically poor job of it, had put her own needs above those of the gods. She was sorry, but she dared not even say that, for fear of further angering the goddess.

"Useless," hissed Yemoja. "Just like your mother."

"No," whispered Ashâke, tear droplets flying from her cheeks as she shook her head. "No. You can't say that. She gave her life—"

"*I* GAVE HER LIFE!" screamed the goddess. "Me! Yemoja! She was dead and I resurrected her and she thwarted my plans. Locked us away for *seasons*!" Her lips peeled back in a vicious snarl. "Do you know how much time we have lost, how grossly disadvantaged we are, only for you to further endanger us by questing after flimsy mortal relationships? You exist because of me. You exist to serve us. And you belong to me."

Perhaps Yemoja was right. The godkillers would not have grown so strong, so formidable, if her mother hadn't interfered. They had had four hundred seasons to infect the world—perhaps even longer, who knew how long they had plotted before the Fall?

Ashâke broke into fresh tears. The other orisha were clustered around her, watching silently as Yemoja berated her. Waves of disappointment emanated from them. Through teary eyes she looked from one to the other, and was met with grim faces. Even Oya, who always had an easy smile for her, looked angry.

"Eh, perhaps it's for the best," said Arewa. "I, for one, find this business of running like mindless sheep rather exhausting. We are simply living on borrowed time. Sooner or later—and I'm really starting to hope sooner—the godkillers—"

"Shut up!"

Yemoja rose to her feet, shedding her mortal form, the tight curls of her hair writhing, writhing, like a million white worms. They swelled around her head like a halo. Her eyes were chips of ice, a blue so bright it was almost colourless. And her voice grew deeper, thunderous with each utterance—

"Do you know your problem? You have lost all reverence. Once upon a time mortals cultivated a proper terror of the orisha. But Olodumare wanted to be closer to you lot, and look what that brought him. Look what it brought us! Now. Now there are fools in Inysha, in all the blasted kingdoms of men, braying for our death! And *you*—do not understand your place."

Yemoja rushed at her.

Ashâke shrank backwards, putting up her arms to shield herself. For one wild moment she thought the goddess would hit her. Smack her across the cheek or deal a blow to her belly. But Yemoja dissolved into blue smoke just as she reached Ashâke, relinquishing her physical manifestation. Ashâke felt her, in the space in her mind where she carried the gods, and for a moment she thought Yemoja was simply sulking.

Then she felt a sharp prick.

Ashâke let loose a terrible howl of agony and dropped to her knees. Pain bloomed at the base of her skull, spreading from one single spot until it seemed her whole head was ablaze. Ashâke grasped her head in her hands, screaming, strings of spit hanging from her lips. She dropped to the ground, thrashing in the grass, and through the haze of agony was vaguely aware of Ogun and Oya and Arewa watching her. She wanted to beg them to help her, but she had no words, could not form words. There was just her screaming. Yemoja was doing something. It felt as though her skin were being *stretched*, her mind *shredded*—

"No!" she gasped, but even that was wrong. She did not speak; her voice rang out in her head. And she understood with a jolt of horror what was happening. Yemoja was trying to take command of her body. She was trying to render Ashâke a prisoner in *her* own mind.

Animal instincts kicked into action. Ashâke's etchings came alive, glowing a blinding blue-white as she wrestled Yemoja: a contest of wills, a desperate act of self-preservation; Ashâke fought the goddess who nipped and snapped at her essence like a wild dog. For she feared what would happen if Yemoja took her over.

Ashâke screamed.

Light sheared from her mouth, from her eyes, from the very core of her being, and she felt Yemoja's forceful expulsion. The goddess appeared, now abandoning every pretence of mortal manifestation and presented in her true form.

She loomed over Ashâke, glowering down at her, a vision of godly might. Tall. Formidable. Terrible.

"Get out of my sight," she thundered.

Ashâke scrambled to her feet and fled. She half ran, half tumbled down the hill, seeking to put as much distance as she could between herself and the gods, but it was like trying to flee one's own skin. The orisha were with her, they were always with her, and Ashâke felt their disgust, their disappointment, dogging her. Hot tears clouded her vision, turned the forest to a wash of green so that she could scarcely see where she ran. Still she ran, stumbling over roots, racking gasps rocking her body. And when she could run no more, she collapsed on the soft soil by a creek and hugged her knees to her chest and wept.

Ashâke wept until the long shadows of dusk turned to night, until the chitter and cricking of nocturnal insects filled the air. She wept until she had no more tears to give, and her hollow, full-throated sobs became weak dry hiccups. Her throat was raw, her heart was raw, and though she was aware of the orishas' presence, she felt wholly and utterly alone. She stared out to the dark creek, watching the black water gurgle over mossy stones and boulders. And because she stared but did not really see, and because she was lost in her own misery, she did not immediately notice that the water was no longer water, but a window, and in it she saw—

She saw *him*.

He was garbed in a red-and-gold kaftan. He radiated a quiet power, the smugness of one who knew he could crush the world in one fist. Seven golden locs tumbled across his shoulders. And he watched her with golden eyes, eyes that burned like twin suns, eyes that seemed to bore into her very soul. He seemed larger than life, even more terrible than the vision the Master Griot had conjured in Song.

"Bahl'ul," she breathed. Terror seized her heart and Ashâke cast about, half expecting Bahl'ul to step out from behind a tree. But all around her were dark trees, and low shrubbery. She was alone in the forest. With great trepidation, heart thudding in her ears, she edged towards the creek and peered into it.

He was still there. This was not some conjuring of her

mind. Somehow the Teacher himself, the killer of the Supreme Father, was here, in the water.

"Do not be afraid," said Bahl'ul.

"No?" she said, voice high and tight with terror. "You're going to kill me."

"Kill you?" Bahl'ul frowned. "No. No, no, no. My quarrel is with the orisha . . . and anyone who would protect them."

"*I* protect them."

"Do you?" He made a show of looking around. "Then why are you here, bawling your eyes out? Might it be because you have only just narrowly escaped entrapment?"

Ashâke's blood ran cold. "How . . . *how* do you know that?"

He smirked. "Come now, Ashâke."

Come now. As though she were nothing but a child who had voiced a foolish question. And she *was* a child—a bumbling, flailing child before this entity, this being who had slayed Olodumare. Bahl'ul was powerful beyond her wildest comprehension.

"I know a great many things. Things you can't even begin to fathom. I know you do not fully understand the power you wield. And that is by design."

"Why haven't . . ." She swallowed. "Why haven't you killed me?"

"You are not listening. Nothing is more precious to me than mortal life. And you, for all that you're the Guardian, are still mortal."

Ashâke frowned. What twisted mind games was he playing? She had known sooner or later she would face him, but this was not what she had expected. Not this open dialogue, as if they were not enemies. It must be a trick. Perhaps he sought to lower her defences, to appear harmless so she would trust him. But she had learned the hard way to trust no one. "You killed my friends," she said. "Slaughtered an entire clan of griots. So how can you claim to care for mortal life?"

Bahl'ul's lips twisted in distaste. "The work of my wayward followers."

"They were looking for me."

"They were looking for the orisha," he said softly. "Crafty, craven creatures who thought they could escape my wrath."

"Why?" she asked. "Why do you want to kill them? Why do you hate them so much?"

"You hate them too, don't you?"

Did she hate them? Yemoja had tried to overtake her. And the others . . . they had simply watched. But she wasn't about to find common ground with Bahl'ul. "I asked you first."

Bahl'ul produced a terrible smile. "Clever. In the beginning, yes. I abhorred them. Now I am . . . beyond hate. Think of me as a servant; mankind's servant. I simply do what needs be done."

"By killing our Creator, destroying all that holds the world in balance?"

"By liberating us from tyranny."

"Tyranny?" Ashâke laughed in spite of herself. "You've made yourself into a messiah, a liberator. But you are not what you think you are. You and your followers have murdered thousands. *Hundreds* of thousands! Is that not tyranny? Surely you know what happened after the Fall? You broke the world! Countless souls perished. And you set loose your dogs on the world. They stole lives, consuming souls just so they could hide in plain sight and do your dirty work." She thought of Iyalawo, of Djola, of the countless nameless people whose souls had been consumed by the followers, whose bodies had been stolen. She thought of Djábri, and hundreds like him who suffered in the presence of their loved ones, hanging on to the impossible hope that the person they loved was still in there somewhere. She thought of Simbi, her best friend, forced to betray Ashâke to save her family. "All so you can kill the orisha, who have done nothing but provide for us. Is that not tyranny?"

"They do not provide," said Bahl'ul. "They do *not* provide. You think them harmless. You think them blameless. You worship them, still. But that is what they are good for, making you believe they are the beginning and the end, that your life matters naught without them."

"It doesn't!" she cried, throwing up her arms. "None of this is possible without them. *You* wouldn't be alive without them."

She had touched a nerve. Rage curdled his features and

the water rose in the shape of hands that seized her behind the neck. Before Ashâke realised what was happening they tugged, and she plunged face-first into the shallows—

She was Bahl'ul. She was Yinka. She felt his pain as he watched his daughter grow sick with each passing day, she knew his desperation as he stole into the Tower and journeyed to Orun, seeking, hoping, to petition the orisha. She balked at the callousness of Shopona, of Yemoja, of the lesser and greater orisha. Their utter contempt for human life. His pain was hers. His grief was hers. His rage *was hers—*

The vision ended and Ashâke found herself on her hands and knees, coughing and spluttering as she gasped for breath. She gaped into the water, which still danced with ripples, looking at Bahl'ul with fresh eyes. "That's why . . ." she gasped. "You do all this for . . . for vengeance?"

He pressed his lips into a grim line. "For mankind. So none would need suffer as I have. So none would need dance to the tune of callous gods. Think about it—you did not become idan of your own volition. You were given no choice, no say, in the matter. The orisha forced you into this role, as is their way."

True, she had been given no choice. Her mother had tried to barter her life for Ashâke's, but the orisha—no, *Yemoja*—had insisted.

"And now they have tried to steal your body, to trap you in your own mind. Don't you see that they are using you merely as a tool? Don't you see that all man has ever been to the orisha is a tool?" He leaned in, his lips almost touching the undersurface of the water. "Don't you see that your life is worth nothing to them?"

Ashâke licked her dry lips. He had a point. Stars above, he had a point. Even Iyalawo had tried to wrest autonomy from the orisha, to direct the path of her own life, to keep her daughter from them. Ashâke *was* a tool, a tool for the survival of the orisha. Hadn't Yemoja said as much? *You belong to me.* They did not see her as her own person. A living, breathing mortal with wants and desires. She had thought herself special but was not, was the furthest thing from special. She had been locked into servitude only because they relied on her for their existence. For the past ten moons she had suffered humiliation at their hands. Did she hate them? She didn't know. But she was tired. Tired of running, of hiding, of answering to their every whim, of being made to feel . . . *less.*

"All you need do is give them up," Bahl'ul whispered, "and my work will be done. You need not die." He stretched out a hand. It hit the undersurface of the water, as though the creek were merely a transparent membrane. "Take my hand. And I will be there."

Ashâke stared at his hand, open in earnest supplication.

"How do I know . . . how do I know you aren't lying? That this . . . vision isn't just some trick?"

"You know it is not a trick. I have shared with you what I have never shared with anyone else. Not even my followers.

And I know you no longer want to be held in thrall by the orisha."

No, she didn't. All she needed do was take Bahl'ul's hand and—"I can't." She swallowed. "If you kill them, if you 'liberate' us from the orisha . . . the world will perish. I've seen it. The forests, the birds, the people. It's all connected . . ."

"Lies!" snarled Bahl'ul. "Lies to preserve themselves. The orisha think the world cannot function without them but it is not true. I am much more powerful than they are, than Olodumare himself ever was. And I will mold the world in my image. I will make a paradise of Aye, shape a world where man need not suffer the whims of callous gods."

"Wouldn't that make you the very thing you seek to destroy? Wouldn't that make you a god?"

Bahl'ul bristled. "I am much more than a god." He stretched out his arms as if to embrace the air. "I am the Great Redemptor."

"I thought you were a servant. Which is it?"

Bahl'ul offered his hand, and there was impatience in his eyes. "Take my hand," he said. "And the strife of countless seasons will be over in a heartbeat—"

The crack of a twig sent Ashâke wheeling around. Yemoja stepped out of the trees.

ELEVEN

Yemoja had assumed her mortal form.

Ashâke glanced back at the water but it was only a creek, the black water gurgling over moss-covered rocks. Bahl'ul was gone, if ever he had been there in the first place.

There came a rustling of leaves as the others stepped into sight.

"We must move," said Yemoja. "The godkillers will know where we are." She started away, then stopped when she realised Ashâke hadn't moved. She hadn't even risen to her feet. "Are you deaf?"

For reasons Ashâke couldn't understand channeling her powers served as some sort of beacon for Bahl'ul's followers, who were no doubt now swarming towards this place, considering there had just been a fantastic display of power as she battled Yemoja. They needed to move, but not before she set some things straight.

Ashâke rose slowly to her feet and faced the goddess.

"You violated me," she said. "Violated my trust. You tried to take my self-will from me. It won't happen again."

Yemoja turned to Ashâke, her face a mask of incredulity. "It won't happen again? Child, do you forget to whom you speak?"

"You are Yemoja, orisha of rivers and fertility, mother of all orisha."

"Then you know that I am not beholden—"

"But you are." Ashâke looked around, meeting each orisha's gaze in turn. "You all are beholden to me. I never asked to be made idan, to share this burden that is wholly yours, but here we are." She beat her breast. "I, Ashâke, am the one thing keeping you all alive, the one person who stands between you and total annihilation at Bahl'ul's hand. You would do well to remember that."

A stunned silence descended upon the clearing. Ashâke heard the heavy thud of her heartbeat in her ears, felt the orisha's emotions: a mix of rage and shock and even grudging admiration, but she could not tell which belonged to who. They all regarded her with open surprise.

Fury curdled Yemoja's features. "You insolent, irreverent—" Her bosom heaved as she struggled for words. "Perhaps I should—"

"Take me? You can try."

Was she not the amalgamation of all the orisha, and, by extension, all their powers? What might they possessed was also hers. Ashâke could channel them all, harness their combined strength, whether or not they liked it. Whether or not they were willing. They had made her think she was nothing, and could do nothing without them. But they had only been keeping her on a leash, when in truth she was the tree, and they were the branches. When in truth it was her roots that dug firm into the deep of the earth.

Ashâke saw the moment understanding came to them, as they realised she had come into knowledge of her true potential.

The faint rustle of leaves sent them all spinning.

"Show yourself!" boomed Ogun, swinging his hammer.

For one tense moment, nothing happened, then the shrubbery quivered as it parted and an armoured figure stepped into the clearing.

"Djábri?" said Ashâke.

Four more figures, three men and one woman, stepped out after him. They wore armour of beaten bronze and boiled leather and that distinct red helmet that marked them as soldiers. But where the Inyshini soldiers had borne bronze swords and spears, these ones bore gleaming weapons of a material that looked at once strange and familiar. On seeing the orisha, the soldiers dropped immediately to their knees.

"Orisha," muttered the woman warrior to Djábri's right. "I bless this day where you've granted me grace to see not one, not two, but four of you. What my baba and his baba have never seen, yet these eyes are fortunate enough to see. I am your humble servant."

Ashâke felt the orisha grow stronger, replenished by even this small act of worship. Yemoja shot Ashâke a quick look, one which seemed to say *see what proper reverence looks like*. She turned away from the goddess. "Djábri. What are you doing here?"

"We saw the light and I recognised it from when you . . ."

"Attacked you." There was an ugly curved scar where he had struck his head against the wall when she thought him her enemy. Ashâke frowned. "But I thought you returned to Inysha. How are you here, so close to Abeokuta?"

"I escaped not long after you left," said Djábri. "Barely. Yaruddin . . ."

The oldest of the lot stepped forwards, a grizzled, battle-hardened warrior. "Forgive me, but do you mean to fight?"

"Fight?"

"Scouts spotted godkillers racing here on horseback. If we are to evade them, we must leave now."

"Of course," said Ashâke. "Of course . . ."

They moved swiftly through the forest. Ogun relinquished his physical manifestation, as did Yemoja. Arewa struck up conversation with the woman warrior, Wunmi, who could not mask her awe, stumbling over her words, eyes flitting from Ashâke, to Arewa, to Oya. Ashâke could not blame her. It wasn't just that the warriors were among the first to lay eyes on an orisha in nearly four hundred seasons; it was that the gods' very presence commanded awe. Ashâke too had been awestruck in the beginning, awestruck and grateful that they had chosen her. Until she grew to know them, their temperament, and now their secrets. Her descent into apostasy had been a slow one, as she realised that the gods were not perfect. They were every bit as flawed and broken as mortals.

They soon appeared in a clearing where the warriors had tethered their mounts, and with swift, silent hand signals they set off. Ashâke rode with Djábri, clinging on to him as they tore through the forest in tight formation. The wind lashed at her and brought tears to her eyes so that she was forced to squint, the forest reduced to a blur around her. And then they were out of the forest and the lofty Mountains of Abeokuta appeared before them.

Abeokuta meant "under the rocks," named for the rocky mountains in whose shadow the city was built. Back in the temple Ashâke had learned from Priest Jegede, an Abeokuta native, that the earth beneath the mountains was rich with minerals; as such the city birthed generations and generations of miners who plumbed the depths of the earth for coal and gold and other wondrous ores. She had heard of their elephants too: majestic, highly intelligent creatures that bonded with their miners, hauling ore-laden wagons out the mines and into the light.

The jagged mountains darkened the horizon: black, toothy projections that loomed like several slumbering giants. The mountains were nigh unscalable from this side, the only way in and out of the city being a tunnel that bored through the base of Omiri, the largest of the mountains. A vast barren expanse led up to the base of the mountains, so the watchmen who lurked at the peaks could spot an approaching army from afar.

"Here they come!" yelled the grizzled captain.

Ashâke cast over her shoulder to the west, where she saw a cloud of red dust: godkillers, cutting from the left, racing to intercept them. Her heart galloped as the memory of her last encounter with them rose in her mind: the acute pain of Simbi's betrayal, the tall flames, the smoke; staggering half-paralysed through the streets, her mind swimming with the delirious cocktail of fear and confusion and the potent high of yeoleaf. Then, she had escaped by the skin of her teeth. She had escaped, thanks to Djábri, who was yet again coming to her aid. Was this, then, her lot? Was she condemned to a life of endless flight, surviving on the mercy of strangers and ardents—the few left who would risk the wrath of the followers? When would they, as Simbi had been forced to, choose themselves, choose their families over the orisha? Over her?

The godkillers were gaining on them; where before they had lagged to the west and behind, now they were neck and neck, cutting diagonally towards them. Ashâke and her party were on one edge of an imaginary arrowhead, and the godkillers were on the other. If they continued on this path they would eventually meet at the tip.

"Signal the gate!" barked the captain. Wunmi fumbled

for the horn at her hip, brought it to her lips, and blew. A caterwaul pierced the air.

Ashâke chanced another glance at the godkillers, who were nothing but shadows in the cloud of red dust, silhouetted against the yellow of a low moon.

The crack of whips rent the air, as each warrior urged their mounts faster. Djábri whipped mercilessly at his steed, screaming "Yah! Yah!" and the poor beast ran, frothing at the mouth, eyes rolling, sides pumping like a bellows as it sought to bear them faster. Each step rocked Ashâke's insides and made her sick with fear. She could not tell where her fear ended and the orisha's began. But it was there, a roiling, nauseous thing. She felt she would throw up—

"How many are there?" cried Wunmi.

"Nine," said Djábri. "No. Ten!"

It was hard to tell their number in the cloud of dust. There could be ten, or twenty. But these were the godkillers who had been in the vicinity when Ashâke channeled. Was Bahl'ul among them? Was he on one of those horses, charging at them? Had he merely been stalling for time while his cronies advanced on their location?

"Captain Doro!" yelled Wunmi. "We need to—"

Her horse let loose an eerily human scream. Ashâke turned to an explosion of hot, wet blood. It got in her mouth and got in her eyes, and when she managed to blink away the red from her vision Wunmi was gone. Twisting dangerously Ashâke saw the warrior and her horse rolling and bouncing in the dirt, fast vanishing in the dust.

Without thinking Ashâke dove off her horse. She landed on her side, tucking into a roll to break the thrust of momentum. A strangled cry tore from her throat as arrows of pain ripped through her body. The wind drove from her lungs. But she picked herself up, wheezing, blinking stars from her vision as she surveyed the field for Wunmi. For a moment she could see nothing at all, could make out nothing through the pall of dusk and dust. Then she glimpsed a shape in the distance. Ignoring Djábri's bellows, ignoring the orisha's screams, Ashâke half limped, half ran towards Wunmi.

The horse was dead. It lay in a ruin, eyes glassy and unseeing, the spear that had killed it still protruding from the mess of gut and viscera. A powerful stink of blood, of wet iron, hit Ashâke in an overwhelming wave and she bit back her gorge. Even as she watched, the spear dissolved into mist as she sidestepped the rapidly calcifying horse to find—

"Wunmi!"

The warrior's eyes focused at the sound of her name, settling on Ashâke. Bloody bubbles popped on her lips as she struggled for breath. "Blessed . . . One . . ." she gurgled.

"You'll be alright," said Ashâke, running her hands over the woman, at a loss for what to do. "You'll be—"

Violent hands seized Ashâke from behind, flipped her around so that she found herself face to face with Oya. "What are you doing?" hissed the goddess. *"Just what do you think you're doing?"*

"Saving her."

"We need to save *ourselves*—"

Djábri came cantering over, reining in his horse so violently it screamed. He slid off the beast in a fluid movement just as the other warriors arrived.

"Help me!" Ashâke yelled at them. "Quick!"

"She's dead," said Captain Doro gravely.

"What do you mean she's—" Ashâke whipped around to find Wunmi gazing sightlessly, utterly still. "No . . ." she whispered. "No . . . no . . ." Tears stung her eyes. She didn't know this woman, had met her less than an hour ago, and now, because of *her* . . .

She was back on the riverbank, stumbling helplessly past dead griots. The wails of anguish, of fear, the guilt that nibbled at her. They were dead. They were all dead because of her.

"Ashâke," began Yemoja, eyes darting from Ashâke to the rapidly approaching godkillers. "Now is not the time—"

"No," she whispered. "I won't put any more mortal life in danger, not on your account. It's me—it's *you* he wants." She turned to the warriors. "Go. Save yourselves!"

But it was too late. The godkillers were upon them. She could see them clearly now; they numbered almost thirty, wearing old skins, young skins, clutching that formidable scimitar that ate through flesh. They set their mounts to a brisk canter as they encircled Ashâke and company, hemming them in like pigs in a pen, ululating as they jabbed with long spears that seemed made of night.

The warriors spread out in a half circle, weapons at the ready, shielding Ashâke from the godkillers. With a cry of fury Djábri charged at the nearest one, slashing the horse's legs. It screamed and bucked, and the godkiller fell to the ground.

With an almighty roar Ogun swung his hammer into the flank of a nearby horse. The beast screamed as it went flying, horse and rider vanishing into the night.

Ogun pounded across the field with a roar, swinging his hammer and sending the godkillers flying. In the past when they had met, the orisha had refused to fight, for fear of drawing other godkillers to their location. Now, with Ashâke bent on serving them up, they had no choice. And they fought for their lives. But what made their lives more precious than that of mortals? They were staying the inevitable.

A grunt of pain sent Ashâke wheeling and she saw Captain Doro plunging his blade into a godkiller's heart; the woman toppled backwards, gurgling, a dark red stain soaking her kaftan. Then she slumped to the ground, dead. *All well and good,* thought Ashâke. But what use was it when the godkillers would simply switch bodies? Even as she watched, purple-black mist, the same kind she had witnessed leaving Yaruddin's first body ten moons ago, what she now understood was the godkillers' ashe, seeped out of the fallen godkiller and enveloped the captain—

An eerie bloodcurdling wail filled the air. Ashâke winced—everyone winced. She slapped her hands to her ears, muffling the inhuman sound that was coming from Doro.

No. From the *mist*.

The ashe quivered as it rose from Doro, rose high into the night sky like smoke from a forge, and Ashâke realised it was fleeing. The godkiller had tried to possess the captain, but had been repelled.

Presently Ashâke's eyes turned to Captain Doro, who stood in a pose worthy of songs, whose visage was one of a triumphant warrior, rendered all the more powerful by the fact that he was lit with a radiant light, for his bracelet, his scimitar, all the weapons on his person glowed a bright yellow-orange, like the sun at sunrise.

Like the object.

Deification

It was raining.

It had been raining nonstop for nearly two days; sometimes it reduced to a drizzle, and sometimes it poured down in torrents, but it always rained. Yinka stood, soaked to his bones, in the vegetable garden behind his hut, staring at the fresh mound of earth that was his daughter's grave. He had been standing there for hours. The truth was he didn't remember coming out here.

After Shopona had finished with him he had flung Yinka out of the sky, where a giant mountain eagle snatched him from his fall and bore him home. The eagle dumped him unceremoniously in the vegetable garden, where he had wept, bawling his eyes out into the grave. Now, several days later, he found that he had no tears.

Yinka looked up at the sky, letting the rain lash his face for a few moments, then he plucked the coil of rope from where he had dropped it and approached the guava tree.

He scouted for a few moments, found a limb just high and sturdy enough to support his weight. With a whoosh he flung the rope around the limb and began to tie a noose.

"Well, well, well," said a silky voice in his ear. "What do we have here? A cliche."

Startled, Yinka looked up to see Eshu perched on the tree limb, hanging upside down so that the orisha's head was right next to Yinka's. He hadn't been there a moment ago, Yinka was sure of it.

"Go away." His voice was hoarse from weeping, hoarse from several days of disuse. "Let me die in peace."

Eshu materialised in front of him. The orisha presented in his human form, and was just Yinka's height. He wore a rough-spun black robe with a deep cowl, but Yinka could just make out his leathery face, the slits of his ruined eyes, the twisted gash of his mouth.

Yinka looked away from him, and continued testing the noose. He had to do this right. He could not botch this attempt to take his own life.

"Your daughter dies," said Eshu. "So you seek to end your own life."

Yinka ignored him.

"'Baa baa baa,'" Eshu mocked. "'I lost my daughter. Baa baa woe is me. Weep for me. The gods are cruel. Look at me I'm so sad—'"

"What do you want?!" Yinka snapped. "Why won't you just—leave me alone?"

"I find you quite interesting."

"You find me interesting?" Yinka gave a bark of mirthless laughter. "What exactly about me do you find interesting? An old mortal broken with grief? A sad man with no desire to live? That you mock me and rub salt in my wounds?" The orisha remained silent, and Yinka blustered on, "But I shouldn't be surprised. I am a simple mortal, and we are merely your playthings. I know that now. It is a lesson hard learned." Yinka gave the noose a tight tug. "So, Eshu, you want 'interesting'? Watch me. Watch me kill myself."

He walked into the shed, where he fetched a chopping block that he placed beneath the tree. He clambered onto it.

"Do you really wish to die? Is that what you want?"

Yinka shut his eyes, taking a deep breath. Then he reached for the noose and settled it around his neck.

"How disappointing," said Eshu, and he managed to *sound* disappointed. "But perhaps I was wrong. I thought the mortal who so boldly stood up my siblings, to Shopona, might show some originality."

Yinka's blood rushed to his one good ear. He had been angry. Enraged. Without a single thing in the world that he cared about. And now . . . he still cared for nothing. His daughter was dead. He had lost all reason to live. So . . . why did he hesitate? Why was he still listening to the whispers of this blasted orisha? He was aware of the rough block beneath his feet, the surface uneven from seasons of chopping wood. All he need do was jump, and—sweet oblivion.

"No mortal has so very bitingly insulted them," said Eshu. "But they've all forgotten. Fickle minds. Even now they're back at their games." He gestured at the sky. "Oya can't be bothered to stop the rain."

Yinka found himself taking deep and measured breaths. He opened his eyes.

"What was it you said?" Eshu stepped closer, and Yinka could not tear his eyes from his lips as he shaped the words. "Petty, oversized children with little regard for human life? Petty, oversized children saddled with immense power. A dangerous combination. How . . . does that make you feel?"

Yinka was panting now, his breath coming hard and fast as he clenched and unclenched his fists. He still couldn't see very clearly out of his eyes; the world had taken on a vague pink hue.

"Yinka, how does that make you feel?"

"Livid," Yinka growled, spittle flying from his lips. "FUCKING INCENSED!"

Eshu smiled. "What if you could have revenge?"

Shopona's cruel voice rang in his ears. *You will spend your days seething with rage, but ultimately helpless, as all mortals are, to do anything about it.* "I can't. I am just a lowly human."

Eshu closed the gap between them. Yinka felt his breath, hot and delicious in his ears, as he whispered, *"Do you want revenge?"*

Yinka closed his eyes. And Enitan's face rose up in his

mind. His daughter, his precious daughter. He saw her as she had been before the ailment, before Shopona wrenched her away from him. Cruel Shopona who had not had the decency to accept his sacrifice, who did not care for her pain and suffering. "Yes," he hissed. "Yes, I want revenge."

Eshu broke into a hideous smile, then seized him.

Yinka gasped as the block vanished beneath his feet. He thought at first the orisha had pushed him, and realised in the moment before his mind caught up to what was happening that he did not want to die. But the noose did not tighten around his throat. In fact, there was no noose. There was just Eshu's arms around him, embracing him in a powerful hug. They were falling, or it seemed they were flying, Yinka could not tell which. The wind roared in his ears and he opened his eyes and let out a small gasp.

They were in a . . . he couldn't tell where they were. Around him stretched the endless night sky, as though he had vaulted the heavens into perpetual night. He could see the stars, sprinkled across the vast tapestry of the cosmos. They looked so much bigger, closer, and though Yinka stretched a hand to touch them he never could. Clouds of colourful smoke—all the colours of the rainbow and more, colours that he had no name for, colours so vibrant they hurt to look at—looped lazily in the air, and it seemed to Yinka that the clouds were alive, for there was no wind to move them. In the far distance, a burst of golden-white light interrupted the monotony of the night sky, a blot in the fabric of the universe, like a window to another world.

Or endless worlds.

"What is . . . what is this place?" Yinka whispered, and his voice carried as though he were in the vast interior of some ancient temple.

"What do you see?"

Where before there was nothing but endless empty darkness, now structures loomed into view. Yinka saw an old hut, with weeds crawling down its crumbling walls; he saw the wooden rack upon which he had hung many a hide to dry; he saw the guava tree where but moments ago he had sought to end it all; he saw a garden, and the lone well in the corner.

"This is my . . . this is my house."

"Ah, so it presents as something familiar to the beholder. Fascinating!"

Except it *wasn't* his house. The structures were there, eerily familiar, but they were wrought of that same stuff of night that made this place, whatever it was.

Yinka turned to Eshu, who was watching him as one watched a curious creature. "Where are we?"

"I don't know," said the orisha.

"You don't . . . what do you mean—you brought me here."

"I brought you here," Eshu agreed. "I also cannot say what this place is. Both things are true."

Yinka groaned in exasperation. "You've said a whole lot of nothing."

"Have I? Maybe you're just not listening."

"I won't get a straight answer out of you, will I? You orisha . . . you're all the same. Cryptic. Especially you, Eshu. You are a liar. And a trickster. I don't know what game it is you're playing but I want no part of it. Take me back."

Yinka had meant for the words to cut, but Eshu could not have looked more unoffended. He walked over to the well and perched on its lip, crossing his legs. "I *am* a trickster, and much trouble I have gotten for my . . . tricks. Once, I plied my father with sweet wine and robbed him of his secrets. He spoke of many things, things my siblings can't even begin to fathom. Secrets he kept closely guarded. My father loved his secrets. But he also loved my mother's wine, and I gave it all to him. In his drunken ramblings he spoke of this place. Where he came from, where he was . . . made. He soon realised what I had done and was not too happy about it. I fled from him, but he found me." He pulled down his cowl and showed Yinka his first face. "First he took my lips, to make sure I would never tell of it, then he took my eyes so I would never find it. You see, roads . . . they don't always stay where they should. They appear and disappear. The world is a coy mistress." He smiled. "But I am lord of roads and crossroads. No path is hidden from me."

A place where Olodumare was made? Yinka had never given a thought to the fact that the Supreme Father had been made. It just wasn't something that crossed his mind. But if this was not some cruel joke, who *made* Olodumare?

"If this is true . . . why would you tell me, a mortal?"

But Eshu had secrets of his own and did not respond. He said, instead, "I have spent an eternity searching for the Fount of Creation."

"The Fount of Creation?"

Eshu gestured at the well upon which he sat.

Yinka walked over with limbs of lead, then peered into the well. Inside was black water, and he caught his haggard reflection on its surface. It looked like ordinary well water, save for the fish. A lone silverlight fish darted around, mouth opening and closing. Before he could stop himself Yinka reached into the water. The surface broke, and the fish fled, plunging deeper into the depths until it was nothing but a point of light.

"Go ahead," said Eshu, already at Yinka's shoulder. "Drink it."

"What happens if . . . I drink it?"

"You get what you want."

Yinka turned his gaze to Eshu. "Have *you* drunk of it?"

Eshu met him with level eyes. "Who says I haven't?"

That was a non-answer. A dozen questions swirled in his mind—why was Eshu helping him? Against his own sibling, no less?—but he would never get a straight answer out of him. The orisha only revealed what he wanted to. Yinka chewed his lips. He could go back, go back to . . . tying his noose. But Eshu had brought him here, and no matter how scared or worried he was that this was some trick, he really, truly, had nothing to lose. And if he ended up getting what he wanted, did anything else really matter?

But what did he want?

Yinka scooped up a handful, and drank.

It felt like . . . nothing at all. It had a texture that almost felt like water. It felt to him like he was drinking air made liquid, or liquid made air.

Yinka opened his eyes to find Eshu gazing at him expectantly. "Should I . . . drink more—ah!"

A tingle in his chest. As though he had swallowed a bird that fluttered about in his rib cage. Then the tingle became unbearable as it turned into a ball of searing heat that scorched the inside of his chest. He staggered backwards, clutching at his breast, at his neck.

"I don't feel . . . feel too good."

Eshu merely watched him with mild curiosity.

"Please—" Yinka gasped. *"Help!"*

Heat flared through his body and he saw lines of light appear in his skin, tiny seams that slowly widened as though he were being ripped apart from within. He *was* being ripped apart from within. The pressure, the heat, built in his chest, in his head, in his belly. Yinka dropped to his knees, heart thudding in his ears, scrabbling frantically at his chest. He ripped off his shirt and clawed at his skin, howling, spitting gibberish. Great gouges appeared where his nails dug into his skin, and from them light burst forth.

Yinka screamed. A great gout of blinding light erupted from his mouth, his eyes, from every orifice in his body. It seared the night, and to the casual eye he might have seemed a beacon, a star. It burned, Obatala's breath, it burned. Yinka did not know that such pain could exist. And he wanted it to stop. All he wanted was for it to stop. He had changed his mind. But words would not come. There was only his scream, raw and primal, the language of agony.

Yinka felt himself, his *mind,* come undone. He was up and he was down. He was here and he was not here. He was pain. He was agony.

The screaming stopped, or perhaps it never stopped. Some time passed, a long time, perhaps a short time, and where Yinka stood there was nothing but a faint wisp of colourful cloud, which floated up and up and joined the rest of the clouds in their celestial dance.

Eshu, the lord of roads and crossroads, messenger of the orisha, trickster god, was nowhere to be found.

TWELVE

The throne room reminded Ashâke very much of the temple's Inner Sanctum. Tall, tapering walls with bas-relief sculptures, a high vaulted ceiling that opened to the night sky and a spattering of stars. Although several torches guttered in sconces, it seemed their orange flames could not quite drive away the gloom and chill of the chamber; shadows leaked from every corner, from behind massive ornamental vases and statues of trumpeting elephants that flanked the ramp to the round table. Every inch of the chamber and by extension the palace was etched out of a singular piece of igneous rock in a remarkable feat of engineering that conspired to produce a foreboding, awe-inspiring atmosphere.

"Blessed One." Oba Ijasa's voice carried across the vast chamber. "I thought you were resting."

The Oba of Abeokuta was a frail old man, with a quivering voice and a watery smile. He was nearly blind, and walked with the aid of a helper, but his wit remained remarkably sharp. A gaggle of chiefs, all old men, all whose names Ashâke had forgotten as quickly as they introduced themselves, were arranged around the table. They scraped to their feet at her approach.

Had she managed to rest? No, not one bit. She still smarted from burns and scrapes, still felt the rush of her flight and fight. Truth be told, she was exhausted. She longed for a good night's rest. But she couldn't rest, not when there was so much at stake. Not when so many things troubled her mind. "Couldn't sleep, Your Majesty."

Ashâke settled into one of the empty chairs. There were four more, ostensibly put there for the orisha who were off in the city soaking in the adoration of their worshippers. The people of Abeokuta had received them with much pomp and fanfare, singing songs to Yemoja and Oya and Ogun and Arewa, casting flowers and anything they could find as they made the procession to the palace. Hands had reached out to Ashâke, faces alight with fervour as they called her *Guardian, Blessed One, idan*. She had found herself frankly troubled by it all, doubly so when she saw the massive statue of herself in the city centre. She did not know what it meant to be worshipped, to be counted *orisha*. Where the rest of the Ten Kingdoms might have forgotten the orisha, turned under the influence of godkillers, Abeokuta thrummed with a fervour that might have been endearing, had Ashâke not known what manner of beings the orisha were.

"Will the orisha be joining us?" asked Ijasa.

Ashâke reached out to the orisha and they appeared, manifesting before the round table to the awe of the gathered. She rolled her eyes.

Djábri and Captain Doro, battle-worn, stood behind the Oba. Ashâke found her eyes tracing those bracelets, the ones capable of repelling godkillers. Perhaps . . . capable of killing them?

"Your weapons," she said. "I had one like that. Well, not a weapon but a piece. We found it in the ruins of Ile-Ife."

Djábri produced the object, setting it on the table. "This saved my life."

He went on to recount how he had found it when he saved her, how he had kept it always on his person because it gave him confidence, granted him clarity of thought; he told how Yaruddin had tried to leap into his skin and had been repelled by the stone, how he had fled Inysha to Abeokuta.

"It is magic," remarked one of the chiefs.

Obviously. "But how do you all have this . . . metal?"

"Silverglass," said a chief. "We've been calling it silverglass."

"How original," muttered Arewa.

"Em . . . our miners hit a strange new ore, by chance," said Ijasa. "We always stop the dig once we reach the fourth crust. But six moons ago, a green prentice went on past the fourth crust. At first we thought it a new mineral. But we could not quite fathom what it was."

"Until Djábri," said Ashâke.

It had been four moons since she last saw Djábri, since he helped her escape Inysha. And had they not spent moons wheeling about in the desert, they would have arrived here before him.

"Yes. When he told us of this piece, we knew the orisha had given us a weapon to protect ourselves."

"As much as I'd like to take the praise for it," said Arewa, studying his nails, "we had nothing to do with it. At least none of us here do."

"Indeed," rumbled Ogun. "I know every mineral beneath the earth. But I do not know this one."

"So where did it come from?" asked another chief.

"The world changed much in the shadow of the . . . Fall," said Ijasa. "Perhaps it is not so strange to think this is a product of that occurrence. A way for us to protect against Bahl'ul and his followers. In any case we have been mining this silverglass to produce weapons. The process is slow, of course. At the moment we can only arm a few warriors. But our goal is to fashion bracelets for every man, woman, and child in the kingdom, keep the godkillers from stealing their skin."

It was a brilliant plan. Having every citizen carry silver-glass on their person would effectively rob the godkillers of their greatest weapon. But that would only be half the battle, when the Ogboni still existed, mortals who had turned against the orisha of their own accord, who would stop at nothing to see Ashâke dead, who would continue to persecute their fellow mortals.

She sprang abruptly to her feet.

"Ashâke . . . ?"

They were all staring at her, even as she gazed into the darkness beyond the pillar. "I . . . I thought I saw someone . . ." A face in the shadows: ruined orifices for eyes, lips sewn shut with copper thread.

Captain Doro snapped his fingers and Djábri marched over to check. He vanished into the darkness behind the pillar, and for a moment Ashâke had the strangest feeling that he would never emerge, that something in there had seized him, but then Djábri strode out, shaking his head. "Nothing there."

Ashâke was still uneasy.

"Ashâke," said Yemoja, "what did you see?"

"It's . . . it's probably nothing."

"We're dealing with a crafty enemy. We need to be sure."

"Abeokuta is perfectly safe, I assure you," squeaked Ijasa. "Nothing and no one gets in without my knowledge. Certainly not into this palace."

"I thought I saw Eshu," said Ashâke finally. "But it's not—"

"Eshu?" Arewa chuckled into his gourd. "That fool is long dead."

"He's alive." It was Djábri who spoke, and it was to him all eyes turned.

"What nonsense do you speak?" asked Oya, after a moment's silence.

Djábri looked around, his hard eyes chips of onyx in the firelight. "I saw him, in Inysha. He . . . attacked me."

More incredulous silence. Ashâke did not know what to think of this. She had never been able to feel Eshu but she hadn't thought much of it; she merely assumed he had perished in the Fall. But . . . what if he hadn't?

"I think we would all know if my brother is alive," said Ogun, with less conviction than he seemed to intend. He looked at Yemoja. "We *would* know if he's alive?"

"Are you sure?" Yemoja asked Djábri.

"I can't forget his face, my lady. His eyes, his lips . . . and . . ." He cleared his throat. "He knew things about me—"

"The farahàn," Ashâke blurted out. "The farahàn mentioned an orisha gave her the . . . silverglass."

"So you think she was referring to Eshu? And he has been roaming about for four hundred seasons?"

"How has he managed to exist without an idan?" Ogun wondered aloud.

The other orisha had to use an idan because Olodumare was dead, and his magic no longer made it possible for them to exist on Aye. So they had created Ashâke, a weaker substitute, concentrating themselves in her person as they once had been concentrated in Olodumare before he split himself.

"Perhaps he has one," said Oya.

"Impossible," spat Yemoja. "You all know what it took to create Ashâke. He couldn't have managed that on his own. But if indeed he gave the farahàn this metal, then he knows things we don't . . ."

They turned as one to the darkness behind the pillar.

Ogun cursed. He rose to his feet, seizing his hammer. "Legba! Why don't you show your craven face? Don't let me come find you—"

A chorus of screams filled the air. They came from beyond the walls of the throne room, beyond the walls of the palace. They came from the city. A jolt of fear spiked through Ashâke's heart. *Godkillers,* she thought. *They've breached the city.*

"Your Majesty." Djábri was peering out past the balcony, whose doors had been open to let in cool evening air. Something about his tone commanded all their attention.

"What?" asked Ijasa. "What is it?

"Perhaps you should see for yourself, Your Majesty."

Ashâke scrambled after them as they filed out onto the balcony that overlooked the sprawling city below.

"Gods," muttered a chief. "Merciful gods. Are those—"

"Locusts," whispered Ashâke. "Flesh-eating locusts."

Hundreds, no, *thousands* of locusts swarmed in a small cloud that blotted the light of the moon and cast a vast shadow over the city. The buzz and hum of their flight sent a feeling of dread sinking into the pit of Ashâke's stomach.

She clutched the parapet, watching in horror as the locusts moved as if of one mind, then stopped, hovering over the finial of the House of Chiefs. Then they began to reform, moving in waves as they arranged into the visage she had seen in the creek mere hours ago.

"It is him," said Ijasa, and he looked about to piss himself. "It is Bahl'ul."

"People of Abeokuta." The Teacher sounded as though he were everywhere. He sounded as though he whispered right in Ashâke's ear. His giant head was a terrifying sight. Ashâke looked down to see citizens pause in their walking, in their running, as everyone stopped to gaze fearfully at the sky. "None of you have ever met me; none of your fathers nor their fathers before them ever met me. But you all know who I am. I exist in your Songs and your tales, a monster to terrify your young; a demon from the very bowels of Apadi who broke the world. But I am neither monster nor demon. Yea, some call me Teacher; some call me Redemptor. But I am, ultimately, Bahl'ul—servant. Once, I was as you all, beholden to the whims of the orisha, until I freed myself of their yoke. And this gift I seek to share with all mankind.

"You cannot know of the callousness of the orisha, but they are selfish and care only for themselves. To them, your lives are worth nothing. In the long past they have preyed upon our love and devotion. And now, once again they prey upon your good nature. They cower behind the walls of your hospitality and misguided devotion. Know that they will sacrifice every one of you to save themselves."

"He seeks to turn them against us," breathed Oya.

"A fine orator," Arewa chuckled as he magicked more wine into his gourd. "I'm almost half-convinced to turn against us."

"Guardian," said Bahl'ul. "I speak now directly to you. You hold the lives of the orisha in your hands, as you hold the lives of every man, woman, and child of this great city. I have seen your heart as you have seen mine. You know what must be done. Give up the craven gods. At the break of dawn, submit yourself to me, beyond the mountains of the city, and I will deal swift justice to the orisha and end all this. If you don't . . ." He let the silence stretch, pregnant with unvoiced threat. "The world has suffered too long. This war has gone on too long, and it ends, one way or the other, at first crow of the cock."

A terrible silence descended upon the city.

The locusts hovered in the air for a moment, Bahl'ul's giant face gazing down at the frightened Abeokutans, then they dispersed, no longer Bahl'ul's face but a cloud of locusts. They flew the way they had come, buzzing over the mountains and out of the city. Ashâke stood, mouth dry, staring at nothing in particular.

"Can he get into the city?" asked Oya. "Will the mountains keep him out?"

"Those are flesh-eaters!" cried a chief. "He doesn't *need*

to get in the city. He'll simply send those things to—to—"

"Then we barricade indoors," said Captain Doro, stepping forwards. "Your Majesty, allow me to disperse criers to the streets instructing every man, woman, and child to remain indoors—"

"For how long? He will outwait us!"

The chiefs dissolved into hysterics, even as the Oba reprimanded them. Ashâke caught only snatches of their conversation. Her mind was on Bahl'ul, and what he had said to her at the creek, and the unsubtle threat he had just made. She felt eyes on her and turned to find Yemoja squinting suspiciously at her. "'I have seen your heart as you have seen mine,'" she said. "What did he mean by that?"

Ashâke looked away, to the rust-coloured roofs, to citizens gathering in the streets. She tried to imagine herself among them, to feel their fear. The terror that had haunted them for years was now at their door, and he was demanding they give her up, give up the orisha, or else . . .

"Ashâke!"

"I spoke to him!" Ashâke snapped. "At the creek, after you tried to . . . he appeared in the water . . ." They were all gazing at her now, faces a mosaic of worry and suspicion and fear. All but Arewa, who looked like he was enjoying himself. Why did she have to be on the defence? She rounded on them. "He showed me everything, alright? He showed me how he begged Shopona to save his daughter, but you all were too busy with your games. He's right. You think nothing of us."

For a moment confusion flitted across Yemoja's features, an expression that was replicated on the faces of them all on the balcony, then recognition flashed in her eyes. *"Him?"*

Next to her, Arewa burst out laughing. He smacked the parapet, braying with genuine mirth. "Oh hohohoho! What poetic justice! The mortal whose daughter Shopona refused to save is—is behind this? He *is* the Teacher? Oh! Oh!" And he broke into fresh gales, pounding the parapet.

Silence ensued as they digested this new revelation. Then Oya found her words. "How did he . . . when did you . . . ?"

"We need to discuss what we must do," said Ogun.

"There is nothing to discuss," said Ashâke. "He has threatened the city. We cannot stay here."

"Then we run."

"No. I'm tired of running." Ashâke clenched her fists, unclenched them. "I'll give him what he wants."

The Oba's eyes went round, his mouth moving silently as he looked around. "Preposterous!" he roared, spittle flying from his lips. "You can't—you *can't* be serious! Give up the orisha? Forgive me, *but have you lost your mind?*"

Ashâke rounded on him. "Would you rather your subjects die, Your Majesty?" She jabbed in the general direction of the mountains. "Bahl'ul has come with an army. With his wretched demon followers. He will massacre the city. They are not shy about killing. And even if you would give up your subjects to protect the orisha, I'm not prepared to do that. I can't . . ." She flashed back to the beach, the dead griots, the tears, the screams. "I can't . . . I *won't* have more mortal lives on my hands."

"Then we fight! This is what we've prepared for." He nodded at the captain.

"I'll rally the warriors, Your Majesty."

Ashâke laughed, mirthlessly. "You really think you can take them. Take Bahl'ul?"

"Then . . . then *you* fight," he cried in exasperation. "You all fight. You've spent all this time running, never confronting them. Surely your combined might is more than enough . . . ?"

"He killed Olodumare," said Ashâke, "and there was none mightier than the Supreme Father."

"She doesn't want to fight," said Oya, her expression bitter. "Bahl'ul has poisoned her against us."

"No," said Ashâke. "I've merely seen you for what you are."

What was it Ba Fatai said? *We do not deserve anything except that which is our lot.* She had had no say in her life. From the moment she was born, her mother had kept her in the temple. And now, the orisha had hustled her from place to place in search of escape, in search of survival. The truth was she was exhausted. She was done living for others. She had taken her lot, succumbing to the wind of destiny. But she was done. She was taking charge of her life.

"And what is that?" asked Yemoja.

Ashâke glowered at the goddess. "Selfish. Callous. Take your pick."

"Vengeance," quipped Arewa, wiping his eyes. "Has there ever been a motive so pure, so righteous?"

"Shopona is dead!" said Oya. "Bahl'ul has had his vengeance."

"He won't stop until you all are dead," said Ashâke. "And I can't say I blame him."

"So you blame us for being what we are?" She took a step towards Ashâke. "Does not the very same wind that cools your sweat tear down your home? Does not the same rain that waters your crops flood your homes? Do you blame *them*?" She grabbed Ashâke by the shoulders and shook her so violently she felt her head would fall off. "We are what we are! We are orisha!"

"Even now you justify yourself—"

"We are what we are!" cried Yemoja, her voice high and shrill. "The Supreme Father made us so. Shopona was the lord of disease. It was his nature, his *prerogative,* to fulfil—"

"To inflict disease? Even on children?" Ashâke shook her off. "It would have cost him nothing to spare Bahl'ul's daughter, to prevent all this!"

"How did this Bahl'ul gain such power? Ashâke— whatever you think of us, whatever you feel right now, think and don't be a *fool*!"

Fool? But of course the goddess could not imagine that she could make informed decisions for herself. She saw Ashâke, as she now understood all gods did, as a lowly mortal. Beneath them. Well, that might have been true, once upon a time. But not anymore. Ashâke threw off the goddess's hands.

Yemoja cast around for help, desperation in her eyes. But there was no help. Not from the Oba or his chiefs, or the other orisha. "If we die, the world dies! You know that!"

"That's a lie. He said that's a lie."

"Are you certain about that? *Are you willing to find out?*"

Ten moons ago Iyalawo had subdued Ashâke, locking her mouth so she could not speak, taking charge of her body so she could not flee. Now, with a single thought, Ashâke did the very same thing to the gods.

"Do not follow me," she said to the gathered. "Do not try to stop me."

The orisha, mute, subdued, marched after her. She felt their anger, Yemoja straining with fury and fear, but Ashâke mastered them. She was idan. She was the Guardian.

INTERLUDE IV

～∾～

The Teacher

He existed in a timeless place, at the beginning and end of all things. He was woven deep into the fabric of that place. And he understood it all. But with understanding came terror, terror of all that knowledge, of secrets the mortal mind was not made to know. But . . . he was not mortal. Not anymore. Yet, he couldn't exist in this state, in this place, for long. Already he could feel himself stretching, the furthest edges of his mind crumbling under the weight of that knowledge, of that omniscience.

He had to take form.

Yinka gathered himself. He felt the power, the power to make and unmake that thrummed through the fabric of this place. A power ripe for the taking. He threw himself towards it. Something caught his attention, caused him to halt his advance: tinkling laughter, love.

Enitan.

She was here. Somehow she was here. He could feel her

soul, her ashe. He could bring her back. All he needed do was reach out and she would return to him, whole and unblemished, resurrected from the dead. They would live as they had. She would grow to be a lovely young woman, with children of her own. He could resurrect her. But Yinka knew he had been given a boon, one he could use only once. He could have his daughter.

Or he could have power.

Yinka hesitated. If he resurrected Enitan, what was to stop the callous god Shopona from afflicting her anew with fresh ailments? He could not mourn her again; her death had broken him. Worse, he had hated his helplessness and impotence in the face of her debilitating illness. It was a feeling he never cared to experience again. Who would save mankind from the tyranny of the orisha? All those countless, powerless souls beholden to their every whim. And here he was, on the cusp of great power. The gods were a canker and he must rid mankind of their yoke. Yinka understood now that this was his burden, his sacrifice. And he would see it to its end. Bringing back Enitan would be selfish, and would help no one. So Yinka turned his back on his daughter, and reached for absolute power.

It came. Powerful, glorious.

Was this what it was to be an orisha? No. He was more. Much, much more.

Once he was sated he cast himself into the world, searching. Eshu had been right: the world was a coy mistress, its paths endless and ever shifting, and Yinka searched for a while, but in the end he found his quarry.

Atop a mountain, at the dark mouth of a cave, the lord of roads and crossroads sat cross-legged, roasting his dinner on a spit.

Yinka took on human form.

Eshu looked up. The fire cast dancing shadows on his first face as he stretched his sewn lips in a sly smile. "Ah. You."

Yinka walked until there was just the spit between them. To think that he had once feared this creature. Yinka could almost laugh.

"You knew, didn't you?" he said.

"Knew what?"

"When I met you at the Gate, you knew my daughter was already dead. You know all roads. You see all paths. You must have seen her soul tread the path of the dead, and *you didn't tell me!*"

Wind howled through the mountain and the fire roared, fat hissing on the spit. "You didn't ask." Eshu shrugged. He cut a strip of meat and popped it in his mouth, munching thoughtfully. "Besides, what does it matter when you've had your vengeance, and stolen her from death's cold embrace?" He made a show of looking around, his face full of guile. "You *did* resurrect her, didn't you?"

Yinka ground his teeth, glowering at him.

"Oh," said Eshu. *"Oh."* And he burst into laughter, slapping his thighs as he was taken by the gales. And to

Yinka it seemed he was back in Shopona's hall, enduring the ridicule of the orisha who thought themselves better than him.

"Even now you think I'm just a tool for your entertainment. Just like your siblings."

"No. I'm nothing like my siblings."

"You are worse. You're the *trickster*." Yinka charged him. But where sat Eshu moments before was nothing but air. He stumbled and fell, springing immediately to his feet.

Seven Eshus stood before him, eyes burning, lips pursed as they spoke in unison. *"You could have brought her back. You could have saved your daughter. But you chose power. I asked if you wanted revenge. Isn't the ultimate revenge bringing your daughter back from the dead? Isn't the ultimate revenge undoing that which Shopona had done? But no. You lusted for power—"*

Yinka backhanded Eshu; he flew off the mountain, vanishing into the darkness. Yinka dove after him, the wind howling in his ears. He saw Eshu tumbling through the air, a blot against the vast expanse of the Endless Sea below. Yinka seized the god by the neck as they crashed onto the rocky beach. He pressed him against a boulder.

"You *knew* I would choose power! You must have known!"

Eshu chuckled. "I cannot see the future. You made your choice, Yinka, and it was wholly yours. Do not seek to cast off the burden of guilt just because you cannot live with it."

"You dangled it in front of me! You knew I wanted to make Shopona pay and you—"

Behind them the sea roared. Sheets of cold salt spray crashed against them.

Yinka forced himself to take calming breaths. "You sought to use me. Fine. You wanted a tool; you have one. But why stop with Shopona, when I can kill you all?"

Alarm flashed in Eshu's eyes. "Wait—"

The boulder turned to liquid behind Eshu, and Yinka pressed the god into its sticky embrace. Eshu struggled, but Yinka held fast, held tight until the rock swallowed him and became solid once more.

"Killing you would be a mercy," said Yinka. "I want you to know that you were the bane of your siblings."

And he pushed the boulder and dumped it into the sea.

THIRTEEN

Hundreds of godkillers dotted the plains. Some were seated in clusters engaged in hushed conversation, others lay stretched out beneath the sickle moon. The air was pregnant with anticipation. Ashâke's sweaty feet slid in her shoes as she walked towards them, the orisha in tow. She had been staunch in her conviction, but now, seeing the godkillers in their hundreds, she wasn't so sure she was doing the right thing. But it was too late to turn tail. So she walked on, concentrating on placing each shaky foot in front of the other. Someone spotted her, and quick as a wildfire word spread through the camp. The followers rose slowly from their sitting and their slumbering and turned to watch her, a pack of jackals observing their prey.

Perched upon a boulder at the head of the camp was the Teacher. Dressed in the same red-and-gold kaftan with gold sash to match his gold dreads, he was here, not some vision in the water, but here in the flesh. He turned at Ashâke's approach, and a slow smile broke across his face.

"We are much alike, you and I," said Bahl'ul. "That is why I knew you would make the right choice."

Ashâke stopped some fifty paces from him, heart thudding in her chest. "I don't know if it is the right thing, but it is as you say. This battle has gone on far too long, and it has to end." She shrugged. "I see no other way."

She forced the four orisha to their knees, facing away from her and towards Bahl'ul. Then she reached into herself, reached deep into the place where the weaker orisha slumbered, and roused them. One by one she made them manifest until they were all of them kneeling before her, blinking like voles freshly exposed to the sunlight.

Bahl'ul approached, looking not at her but at the orisha, his features lit with an expression of barely restrained triumph.

"Mighty gods!" he crowed, then turned to his followers, pointing at the orisha. "Look what has become of them. Look what has become of the mighty orisha! The craven orisha!"

The godkillers erupted in jeers, hooting and ululating into the morning air. This carried on for a few moments before Bahl'ul held up his hand to quiet them.

"Four hundred seasons I have dreamed of this moment," he said. "Four hundred seasons you have eluded me." He stalked over to Yemoja, then cupped her jaw in one hand, forcing her to look up at him. The expression on her face was scorching, and if she were free she clearly would have attacked him, but Ashâke held her, held them all, under her iron grip.

"Aaah," said Bahl'ul, evidently enjoying himself. "It seems the great mother of the orisha would like to unburden herself." Eyes still on Yemoja, her jaw still in his hand, he said to Ashâke, "Let her speak."

"I remember you," spat Yemoja, once she could speak. "You were nothing but a bumbling mortal when last—"

Ashâke gasped, momentarily disoriented, and it wasn't until she saw the tip of Bahl'ul's scimitar erupt from Yemoja's spine that she realised what had happened.

Then came pain. A white-hot tongue of fresh agony flared through Ashâke's body. She could not tell when she hit the ground, writhing. Darkness seeped into the edges of her vision. Her whole body was on fire—her *soul* was on fire. Someone was screaming. It might have been her, but she wasn't sure. And when she opened her eyes, focusing through the haze of agony, she saw Yemoja disintegrate around Bahl'ul's scimitar, the goddess's physical manifestation breaking off into a thousand glowing flakes that were carried on the dry breeze.

Ashâke lay on the flat of her belly, paralysed with pain, tears leaking from her eyes. Her cheek was pressed against the hard, cracked earth as she watched Bahl'ul—Bahl'ul, whose expression was one of pure rapture. He arched his back as a bright blue light effused out of what remained of Yemoja, rushing into him.

He's absorbing her essence. The thought sheared through Ashâke's mind, cleaved through the fog of pain and shock and fear. Hadn't she seen something similar in the griots' Song? Hadn't she seen the moment Bahl'ul plunged his blade into Olodumare and absorbed his essence? Bahl'ul was a leech, a parasite. He did not just seek to end the orisha, but to take their powers for himself!

Yemoja, the goddess of fertility and seas, Yemoja, the mother of all orisha, was no more. Ashâke did not need to look at the now empty spot where she had been to know; she felt it in her soul—an emptiness, a loss, as though a bit of her person had been chopped off.

A cold realisation came to Ashâke: the gods couldn't be killed without her dying. In the making of her, in making her idan, they had grafted their very essence to her soul, bonding them in life and death. Ashâke did not want to die. Stars above, she did not want—

Bahl'ul, brimming with freshly absorbed power, turned to Ogun. He seized the god of war by the beard, seized him as though he were nothing more than a wild ass, and pressed the tip of his blade in the soft flesh just beneath his chin.

"Wait . . ." Ashâke gasped. She managed to push up on one trembling arm, spittle flying from her lips with the effort, then collapsed back to the ground. "Wait . . . please . . . I'll die."

If Bahl'ul heard her, he paid no mind.

"You promised . . . to spare me."

Bahl'ul looked at her, and there was only a vast emptiness in those eyes. "I lied."

Trust. The great folly of her life. She had trusted Bahl'ul, and now here she was, at his mercy. No one had forced her to give up the gods; no one had forced her to serve up herself like a sheep at the altar. Fool, she was a fool—

A scream rent the air. Ashâke braced for the pain, for the agony that accompanied the death of a god. But it never came. She swivelled her head, gawking at the spectacle before her, for it wasn't Ogun who was screaming but—

A godkiller. He was ablaze, beating desperately at the glowing arrow in his chest, an arrow that burned so bright it resembled a sliver of sun. He danced around, frantic, screaming in ancient Tessini. Then he dropped right in front of Ashâke, as suddenly unmoving as a puppet whose strings had been cut.

They all watched the flames consume his body, the stink of sizzling flesh rife in the air. This was no ordinary fire; the man was already so charred he might have been a log of wood, carved in the vague shape of a human. Even as she watched, the godkiller's soul leaked out of the body, attempting to escape, but was sucked towards the arrow protruding from the chest, where it was promptly vaporised.

The godkillers scattered; someone let loose a guttural cry of "Take cover!" the same moment the wail of a war horn pierced the morning air. Then came drumbeats, synchronised and apocalyptic, and the morning sky darkened as a hail of arrows came raining down. They found their marks, taking the gathered godkillers in the chest and head and throat, each one of them bursting into flames as a hundred glowing arrows struck them, several dozen screams lighting the morning air in a deathly chorus.

Ashâke rolled over, began to scrabble on her arms and belly towards a boulder, towards cover. There was chaos all around. Several flaming figures raced past her, screaming at the top of their lungs; still others huddled beneath tents, beneath fallen horses, sheltering from the rain of arrows. She needed to get out of here. Where was Bahl'ul? Where were the gods? She had thought sacrificing the gods would save mortals. But Bahl'ul had lied to her, who was to say he would stop with the gods? Who was to say he hadn't been so corrupted by a quest for vengeance that he could, would, ever stop? They needed to fight. She reached out to them—

Ashâke felt the ground beneath her tremble as though in the throes of a quake and moments later a mighty elephant charged from the darkness. She rolled away just in time to see the beast crash into the horde, trumpeting as it sent godkillers flying. Several burning bodies hung impaled on its long tusks. A chorus of bellows rocked the air and the ground shook and Ashâke saw warriors pour forth from the darkness.

There were hundreds of them: clutching weapons of silverglass, bedecked in armour of silverglass, each one of them glowing as bright as the morning sun. They glowed so bright that they hurt to look at, dazzling Ashâke as much as they dazzled the godkillers, who, blinded, fell to warriors' swords and spears and arrows. The elephants led the charge, crushing and stomping and flinging everything in their path. Each beast bore on its back a palanquin of four warriors who loosed arrows at the godkillers; bringing up the rear was the cavalry, cutting and slashing and hacking from horseback.

Ashâke staggered to her feet, stupefied. She had left the city ostensibly to save them, but the people of Abeokuta would not give up their gods so easily. Instead they had come to engage in battle. Ashâke nearly wept from relief.

A shadow fell over her, and she looked up to see Ogun silhouetted against the sky. He clutched his bloody hammer in one large fist. For a moment she thought he would use it on her, and she wouldn't blame him if he did.

"I'm sorry—" she said.

He pushed her violently aside, swinging his hammer in the same movement—it smashed into an elephant that had been flying straight for them. The beast crumpled against the iron, then crashed to the ground, a barely recognisable mess of meat and blood.

Beyond the elephant's broken carcass Ashâke saw Bahl'ul. He stood some fifty paces from them, staff held aloft as he moved his lips silently. He was looking straight at Ashâke and Ogun, murder in his eyes. Around him raged a fierce battle, but in his immediate vicinity was a clear circle, as though an invisible bubble protected him, shielded him from the mayhem beyond.

"What is he . . . oh . . ."

A great buzzing filled the air. Ashâke turned with dread towards the sound, to the eastern sky, where it seemed a dark and heavy rain cloud was rushing towards them.

"LOCUSTS!" someone screamed. *"LOCUSTS!"*

"I fear those are not ordinary locusts," said Ogun.

Oya and Arewa appeared next to Ashâke. The three orisha looked at her. And in their silent regard she heard the unvoiced question loud and clear: *What do you want to do?*

Ashâke could tell they were spoiling to join the fight. But she could not let them out of her sight, for fear of Bahl'ul, or even one of the followers, killing them. The thought of fleeing, very briefly, flashed through her mind. But she quelled the traitorous thought. What kind of person would she be if she abandoned these people to Bahl'ul and his ilk? They fought valiantly but the enemy had the numbers, and now that she looked closely, not all of them had silverglass. And even those that had silverglass were not immune to flesh-eating locusts.

Ashâke lifted her hands to the sky. "We fight," she said, and summoned the wind.

A howling wall of wind came from the west. Ashâke was on the ground, in her body, and she was in the wind, she *was* the wind, battering the locusts—

—at the same time she was aware of Bahl'ul's approach. He advanced, slowly but surely, towards them, his bubble cutting through the chaos. She saw the battlefield from above. She saw herself, etchings aglow, surrounded by Oya and Ogun and Arewa, who were wreathed in cords of blue-white light that wound across their arms and bound them all them together—

—Bahl'ul was close now, less than ten paces away. He produced that wicked scimitar and glided straight for Ashâke—

Arewa hurled himself in front of Bahl'ul's blade.

"NOOOOOO!" screamed Ashâke.

Arewa looked from the blade in his chest, to Bahl'ul's snarling face, to Ashâke. A light smile played on his lips as he gasped, "It's all futile, anyway," then disintegrated into a mass of swirling flakes.

Ashâke felt Arewa's essence rush into Bahl'ul and in the moment before he ceased to exist, she saw everything.

She saw Eshu spirit Bahl'ul to the Fount, saw him drink from the Fount. She saw the moment he turned his back on his daughter—

The locusts swarmed them.

Ashâke conjured a small storm that kept the locusts away from her. And in the eye of the storm there was an eerie silence, as though the world had been muffled by a giant hand. Beyond, a tornado of locusts, beating against her stormwall, each buzzing insect spinning and spinning and spinning. Her breath came hard and fast, too loud in the silence. She stumbled over broken bodies, mangled bodies, burned bodies. She stumbled past upturned wagons with wheels creaking into the silence. Dead elephants, calcified elephants. The remains of a warrior whose body had been picked clean. She retched.

"Show yourself!" she screamed. Her head swirled with shock, with revelations—Eshu. Eshu. *Eshu* was behind it all. There came the constant thump thump thump of war drums, or perhaps the thunder of a hundred fleeing feet. Chaos. So much chaos—

Bahl'ul broke into her bubble and then he was before Ashâke, saying, "I have you now, Guardian." He seized her by the throat and stabbed—

Someone wrapped their hands around Ashâke from behind and then she was falling into darkness, away from the battlefield, away from the locusts.

Away from Bahl'ul.

FOURTEEN

Ashâke opened her eyes. Tall, grey-white trunks twisted into the air, huge limbs knitting to form a dense canopy that blocked the night sky. The stench of rot, of old foliage was rife in the air. Ashâke recognised this place, had spent countless nights stealing here to build her idan.

She was in the Sacred Grove.

Someone stepped out from behind a tree. He wore a simple garment knotted over his left shoulder, and he stared at her through unseeing eyes, a slight smirk playing on lips sewn shut with copper thread.

Before her stood the architect of this whole affair. He had taken Bahl'ul to the Fount, given him the means through which he gained unimaginable power—a power that broke the world and sent them all down this path. A power that ruined her life. Yet here he stood, smirking as though this was all some game.

"You!" she snarled.

"Me."

Ashâke sprang to her feet and lunged for him but her hands closed around air. She stumbled forwards, thrown by the force of her momentum. She whipped around to find Eshu leaning casually against an anthill.

Ashâke charged at him, screaming and cursing, but Eshu was no longer at the anthill.

"We really don't have time for this." Eshu's voice came from behind her. He was perched now on a low branch, legs crossed, drumming his fingers on the cracked bark.

"Why?" she asked, panting. "Why did you do it? This is all your fault!"

"Is it really?"

"You offered Bahl'ul revenge! You—you gave him power! Don't play the fool, now, Eshu. You knew what you were doing."

Eshu cocked his head. "And what was that?"

"Sowing chaos!"

"Ah, come now, Ashâke. Things are rarely so cut-and-dried. Have you considered that this was all meant to be?"

"So none of this is your fault? You're merely . . ."

"We are tools at the hand of the universe," Eshu whispered. "We are all merely actors in a cosmic play. Even orisha. The fate of the world is carved in stone; we might try to stay it or alter the path, but fate will be made manifest."

Moons ago, when Ashâke was incarcerated in the larder beneath the temple, Ba Fatai had said something similar to her. *You are not shown the future to alter it, because you cannot. You may try, you may delay it, but the future will be made manifest.* Was all this, then, futile? Were they all doomed to destiny? Ashâke refused to believe that, that she was not in control of her own life. That her actions mattered naught and nothing she did could change the destination set out for her.

"One thing I know," said Ashâke, biting off each word, "is that you're full of mischief and cunning. Your Father is dead, your *siblings*—"

"You offered up my siblings, I think," said Eshu. "You were only too happy to let them die. Of course, that was before you realised that meant *your* own death."

Ashâke glared at him, grinding her teeth. She had been played for a fool. Bahl'ul had shown her just enough to turn her against the gods. That, and Yemoja's attempt to take over her body and mind had filled her with righteous anger, and set her against the gods. Of course she hadn't been privy to the rest of the story, had been oblivious to the fact that Bahl'ul had had the chance to resurrect his daughter, but had chosen instead to go on this crusade. She had been played by Bahl'ul. Played by the orisha. She was merely a pawn in a long cosmic game. And now, whatever Eshu's designs . . . she would not let herself be a part of them.

"What do you care?" she spat. "It all matters little to you."

Eshu touched a hand to his heart. "You wound me, dear Guardian. *Of course* it matters. It all matters."

Ashâke did not believe him, did not believe a single word that came from those lips. She would be a fool to. "Yet here you are, alive. You walk around Aye without need of an idan. Bahl'ul bound you—how did you manage to escape your prison?"

"You ask the wrong question."

"Listen here, you—"

"A much better question would be 'What is this place?' perhaps even—'*Why* am I here?'"

Ashâke frowned, looking around. "This is the Sacred Grove."

Eshu smiled. "Behold"—he waved a hand, gesturing at the Grove at large—"the Fount of Creation."

"What do you mean, the Fount?" Ashâke had seen the Fount in the corrupted planes of Bahl'ul's mind, and it had resembled a well in his garden. But . . . hadn't Eshu said the Fount presented itself as something most familiar to the beholder? She cast about the Grove for an anomaly. The tree before her had been destroyed in a blaze of fire, and yet here it stood whole and unblemished. And the river—

"Oh . . ." she breathed.

With wobbly steps she walked over to the river and peered in. It resembled the night sky made liquid, and in its ethereal surface she caught her reflection.

Eshu was already at her side, and he whispered, "What do you want? What do you want the most in the world?"

Ashâke looked at the river as it flowed silently over the stones.

There are only choices, and the consequences of our choices. Simbi had said this to her long ago. She wanted to be free. She wanted for this all to end. She did not want the responsibility that came with being idan. She wanted to go someplace far where she would never know pain, or sorrow, or fear.

But what would become of Aye and its broken peoples? She had seen Bahl'ul's heart, and she knew his intent. He had boasted that he was much more than the orisha, much greater than the Supreme Father ever was. Did she dare abandon mankind to Bahl'ul and his followers?

"Is this another of your tricks?" she asked. "Am I just treading another path set in stone?"

When there came no reply, she looked up, wheeling around the silent Grove in search of Eshu. But he was nowhere to be found.

FIFTEEN

Under the glare of the morning sun, the carnage of battle revealed itself in all its terrible horror.

The battlefield was littered with the corpses of man and beast alike. Several lay picked clean of flesh and sinew by locusts, leaving nothing but grisly bones like the abandoned props of a macabre troupe.

Ashâke hovered above the field, incorporeal. Not a single living soul was in sight. She feared Bahl'ul had massacred the entire city. She wouldn't put it past him. But then she moved into the city proper, and saw what remained of the Abeokutans.

They had been corralled into the city centre, like hogs in a pen. Grief and fear hung heavy in the air. A dark shivering mass carpeted every surface so that it seemed every roof and wall, the very ground itself, heaved. Bahl'ul's locusts. They were slow and swollen, gorged on human flesh.

The man himself sat atop an elephant, coaxing the beast through the crowd as he addressed the Abeokutans.

"A new dawn is upon us! My work is done. So bury your dead, but know that they died for an empty cause. Your Guardian, your orisha are dead—"

"May they live a thousand lives!" someone screamed. Ashâke cast around for the source of the voice. Her heart faltered. Ralia. The girl was hanging off a window ledge and pumping a fist into the air as she screamed the griot chant for the dead. She seemed to have grown so much in ten moons. And there was a new defiance to her. Gone was the playful child Ashâke had known, the girl who had taught her to play Jagu-Jagu; in her place was one who had seen what no child should. One who had survived the horrors of the world.

A hand reached out from the crowd, and Ashâke saw Ireti, Mama Agba's sister, yank Ralia off the ledge and into her embrace. She pressed the girl's face into her bosom in a protective gesture, ostensibly to stop her from screaming, ostensibly to shield her from Bahl'ul's roving eyes. But it was too late; a clump of locusts detached from a nearby wall and shot for them.

Several pops went off as the locusts exploded, raining to the ground in broken bits and pieces. Just as Bahl'ul brows furrowed in confusion, Ashâke appeared between the Abeokutans and Bahl'ul.

Scattered gasps rippled through the crowd, followed by incredulous proclamations of "The Guardian," and "She's alive!" But none were as shocked as Bahl'ul, who spent a long moment gawking at Ashâke as though she had risen from the dead.

In a way, she had.

"How?" he croaked, finding his words at last.

"You hate the orisha so much, you boast that you are more than the Supreme Father himself ever was." She shrugged. "Maybe you are. But did you not come into your power with the help of an orisha? You would be no one, long returned to dust, if not for the intervention of an orisha."

Fury flashed across Bahl'ul face. That confirmed everything Ashâke suspected, everything she now knew: that he was a man, never mind what powers he now possessed, but he was a man consumed with hubris. He apparently had not revealed this knowledge to his followers. That would tarnish the image he had cultivated in their minds, the image of a messiah come to right the ills of the world. *Understand your enemy,* Yemoja had once told her, *and they lose all power.* She knew Bahl'ul. She understood him.

Bahl'ul's lips curled. She watched his face as he tried to work out how she could possibly know what she knew. After all, he hadn't revealed to her how he came into power; he had been careful to show her just enough to rile her up, to turn her against the orisha and tip her to his side. She saw the moment understanding came to him. "That sly trickster."

"Tell them, Bahl'ul. Tell them how Eshu made you who you are."

"He did not. That fool had his own agenda. He sought to use me for his games, but I am wiser. I outwitted him."

"He provided you with a means to resurrect your daughter, but you didn't. You chose power. Was that not the point of your journey to Orun? To beg Shopona for the life of your daughter? And when you had it, when you had all that power to right that wrong, you didn't."

"For the greater good."

"No, Bahl'ul," said Ashâke. "Because you were selfish. You lusted for power. There are only choices, and the consequences of our choices." She addressed the godkillers, who had listened raptly to this barrage of revelations, and were now looking at Bahl'ul with fresh eyes, with expressions that looked dangerously close to betrayal. "Your Teacher has told you of the sanctity of his crusade, he has convinced you that your cause is a righteous and just one. But it is all a lie. Built on a lie."

"You dare—" Bahl'ul began.

"I dare tell the truth? Yes, Bahl'ul. It was Shopona who took your daughter, but you did not kill him, did you? You went, instead, for the Supreme Father. You sought to take his place."

"So what if I did?"

"Teacher?" It was a bald godkiller with a brass earring who spoke.

"Silence, Vashek," snapped Bahl'ul. He angled his staff at Ashâke. "And you—"

"Why don't you tell your followers the truth, Bahl'ul?"

"I am not beholden to them, nor to you."

Ashâke smiled. "Funny," she said. "Now where have I heard those words before? Ah, yes. It was Shopona who said that to you, wasn't it? You see, Bahl'ul. It is not I who has waged a war against man and orisha alike. You are not a god or a Teacher or a Redemptor or whatever you want to call yourself. You are a small, vindictive man."

Arewa had told of how Koriko, in her fury, trapped Eshu in a tree. So Ashâke dropped to her knees, placed her hands to the ground, and commanded the earth.

But the earth was not the wind; it was old, slow to move, and resistant to change. She threw herself into the vast, stifling darkness of the earth, the battlefield upon which they stood, and she reminded it of what it had once been, of the life it had once harboured. Once, the proud roots of trees had found support in its warm embrace as they climbed high into the sky; once, worms had turned in its topsoil, and enriched the land; once it had lapped up the blood of game, a sacrifice to the sacred existence. Ashâke reminded the earth of all this.

The earth remembered. She felt just the slightest give in its permanence, of what it had been when it had been part of the sister islands, when they had been one, before the Fall. And Ashâke found what she was looking for. The dried roots of an iroko. She seized them, and with a single word spoke life to them:

Grow.

The roots sundered the earth, growing, growing, each gnarled root connecting into a larger root that became a larger root that broke the surface of the earth. Ashâke gasped, thrown backwards. Seven massive roots erupted from the ground like giant serpents. Houses broke apart, crumbling into heaps. The roots caught Bahl'ul, looping around his arms and midriff, and he rose with them high into the air, a fly in a spider's web, as they thickened around him, thickened into a vast, twisted trunk that imprisoned him.

Surprise flashed across Bahl'ul's features, then fear, then fury as he was swallowed by the grey-green trunk of the iroko. The tree continued to grow, higher and higher until Ashâke had to crane her neck to see its top. And when it seemed it would grow right into the heavens, it spread out its branches, each limb bursting with yellow-gold leaves that formed a beautiful corona that shadowed the land.

A great thunder arose in the square. It took Ashâke, who was still on her knees, arms planted to the earth before the tree, a moment to realise it was the sound of rejoicing. Fifteen thousand voices lifted as one in merriment. The sound thrummed deep in her chest and shook the very earth and the locusts, disturbed from their perch, took lazily to the air.

They buzzed higher and higher, away from the congregated Abeokutans, away from the now imprisoned being who had once mastered them, and out of the city.

Someone came running at Ashâke just as she pushed to her feet. They crashed into her, hugging her tightly, and it wasn't until she smelled the coconut oil in her bushy hair, it wasn't until she heard her screams of "You did it! YOU DID IT!" that she realised it was Ralia.

"He said you were dead and I knew he was lying!" cried Ralia breathlessly. There were dried tear tracks cutting through the grime of her face, but her eyes twinkled with delight. "I told everyone, I told all my friends that—" She broke off, a crease in her brows.

"What is it?"

"Your skin . . ."

Ashâke peeled away from the girl as she inspected herself. Slowly, she ran her hands over her arms and face, over every inch of exposed flesh, noting with mild astonishment that her skin was smooth once more. For the first time in ten moons, for the first time in her long life, really, for Iyalawo had merely hidden them from sight, no etchings marred her brown skin, no sacred godscript bound the orisha within her.

"How?" asked Ralia.

"I am not the Guardian any longer."

Ralia looked from Ashâke to the tree and back to Ashâke, evidently puzzled. "Then how were you able to . . . do that?"

Ashâke smiled. In that place beyond the edge of the world, which was, perhaps, the beginning of the world, she had made a choice—although she wondered how much of a choice it was when it was Eshu who brought her to the Fount in the first place. Still, removed from the rest of the orisha she had been certain Bahl'ul had killed them. And everything they had feared would eventually come to pass: rain would cease to fall, wind would cease to blow, the seas would dry and the crops would wither, and the world would perish without orisha, without the beings who lorded over every aspect of creation. So she had chosen to become Supreme. If Olodumare had been the Supreme Father, then she was merely reclaiming his disparate parts, welding them once more into one being. Her. No longer was she Ashâke, humble acolyte, yearning for the voice of the gods. No longer was she idan, tool and Guardian of the gods. She was Olodumare. She was Creator.

Ashâke was drawn to a commotion some twenty paces from her. The citizens had corralled the godkillers into a circle, hemming them beneath the shadow of Ashâke's statue. Many clutched stones, others clutched whatever makeshift weapons their hands could find: cooking pans and metal bars and tree branches, which they chucked at the godkillers, keeping a good distance from them, for they still bore those wicked scimitars. The godkillers slashed, cutting down the crude weapons from the air. But it was an onslaught and many of the projectiles gained purchase, opening deep gashes on foreheads and arms. Even as Ashâke watched, several warriors fought their way to the front of the crowd, placing themselves between the godkillers and the rest of the citizens. And though they were weaponless, their armour and weapons and, most importantly, silverglass surrendered in the wake of battle, they still outnumbered the godkillers.

"Your master is gone!" barked Djábri. "Surrender your weapons."

"If you want it, boy," snarled a woman, brandishing her scimitar, "come get it!"

A tense moment passed in which they faced off, warriors and citizens against what was left of the godkillers, who glared in defiance. Then, Vashek released his scimitar: it fell, dissolving into mist before it reached the ground. In the same movement he reached into his robes and produced a dagger, which he drew across his own throat. He collapsed against a pile of rubble, kicking and spasming. Blood sprayed from the wound, turning the tan of his kaftan a deep magenta. A terrible hush, a shocked hush descended upon the gathering and the only thing to be heard was the disturbing gurgle of the godkiller. He gave one final kick, then grew utterly still. Out came his ashe, the purple-black mist leaking from the body. It rose high into the air.

In equally smooth and silent movements the remaining godkillers took their lives, drawing blades across throats or plunging them into bellies. And their ashe rose like plumes of smoke from some wretched fire.

"Hide!" someone screamed. "They're trying to Eat us!"

Panic spread through the crowd and Ashâke saw the beginnings of a stampede as they scrabbled away, some looking for any piece of silverglass they could find, others diving for the nearest shelter. But the ashe were not attempting to possess bodies; they were fleeing.

It was effortless, catching them. Ashâke seized the souls of the godkillers, shuddering as she felt the stain of their corruption. Holding their ashe was like looking upon another's nakedness, and she longed to rid herself of them. More importantly, she saw that there was no repentance in them.

To the dark with you, she thought as she drove them into the tree.

SIXTEEN

In the Grand Square tables and chairs had been brought out of homes, and they brimmed with hastily cooked dinner. It seemed, in the wake of such an experience, no one wanted to remain alone indoors. Indeed, there was something to be said for shared experience, which brought the smallfolk even closer together. Ashâke watched as families shared food, as strangers exchanged heartily the contents of their cookpots. The air was thick with the smells of pounded yam and efo riro, of moin moin and eko, of beans and corn. The air thrummed with laughter; laughter that was loud and laced with relief. Laughter that rang with an undercurrent of sadness, for victory had come at a cost. But camaraderie was a thread that wound tight around each Abeokutan, and strengthened the bonds that already existed between them. It reminded Ashâke of the griots she had stumbled upon what seemed like seasons ago.

Ashâke watched them all, burdened with the weight of all she knew.

A grand burial ceremony would be held eventually, but Abeokutans never let their dead lie unattended too long. And so much of the morrow would be given to loading their dead onto elephant-drawn wagons to be interred in the crypt beneath the second-largest mountain. There would be some debate over what must become of the charred bodies, for those had belonged to godkillers who had fallen to weapons of silverglass. Some will argue to leave them to rot on the field beyond the borders of the city; and yet others will argue that the bodies had belonged first to people; innocent, ordinary people whose lives had been stolen, and who deserved at last some form of dignity. In the end it would be decided that these bodies be buried on the field where they had fallen, an obelisk with the epigraph TO THOSE WHO GAVE THEIR SOUL AND BODY FOR THE LIBERATION OF MAN. MAY THEY LIVE A THOUSAND LIVES erected in their memory.

Oba Ijasa will send out criers to spread word of Bahl'ul's defeat, and griots will make Songs of all that had transpired. Ashâke knew the Songs would spread far and wide, and would endure for a long time. She knew, also, what would become of Abeokuta: where Ile-Ife had been the first city, the capital city of that old world wrought by Obatala himself, Abeokuta would become the new first city, the new capital, and its name would take on new meaning. It would endure for many seasons. She knew that Djábri would be put in charge of hunting down the remaining godkillers and he would spend the rest of his days carrying out that task. It would be a long process. The battle was won, but Bahl'ul had wrought great discord, and the scars ran deep. It would take a long time to undo the damage he had done. Ashâke knew a great many things, saw very clearly what was to come, which was why she knew she couldn't remain here. She would never see these folk again. Not Simbi or Ralia or Ireti. Not all the tired and sad and hopeful faces of the Abeokutans. Not in this life, at least. So she laughed with them, and made merry. She looked at each of them in turn as she inscribed the moment in her memory, one she would keep forever close to her breast. And though she delayed that inevitable moment of her departure, she would slip away before the crow of the cock. She now understood Olodumare all too well. His yearning for camaraderie. But she would not repeat his mistakes. She understood, at last, her lot.

"Where are you going?" asked Ralia as Ashâke pushed to her feet.

"I'm just taking a walk."

"I'll come with you." Ralia started to rise.

"No, dear one. Sit and eat your food. I'll be back, I promise."

The streets were lit with lamps that illumed the sea of faces and Ashâke wove her way past tables, offering warm smiles to those who called out to her, touching their hands. When she had walked some distance from the city centre, in the quieter and empty residential area, she stopped, turned, and spoke into the darkness. "Is your plan to keep following me?"

Simbi stepped out from the shadows. She looked gaunt, and her nose was crooked, not quite fixed from the blow. *From the blow I gave her.* She stood some five paces from Ashâke, fidgeting with the frayed ends of her shawl. How small, how . . . diminished she looked.

"I know—" Simbi swallowed. "I know you will never be able to forgive me—"

"Forgive you?" said Ashâke, frowning. "*You* are asking for forgiveness?"

Simbi's lips trembled, her eyes glassy with unshed tears. She blinked, and a single fat tear slid down her cheek. "I . . . I thought . . ." She spun on her heels and started to flee.

"Simbi!" In two long strides Ashâke closed the gap between them and twirled her around. "I have no forgiveness to offer you, because that would imply a wrong has been done, that there is restitution to be made. Djábri told of all you suffered, of all your family suffered on account of me, on account of the orisha." Slowly, Ashâke took Simbi's hands in hers, peering earnestly in her eyes. "*I* beg your forgiveness."

Simbi's face fractured in a look of puzzlement. "I don't understand . . . I betrayed you."

"No. You were put in an impossible position. I am not a mother; cannot begin to fathom what it means to be a parent. But my own mother defied the orisha to save me.

She faced Yaruddin, and died by his hands, to save me. Even Bahl'ul did all he could to save his daughter. Who am I to fault you, or blame you, for doing the right thing, for choosing *your* family?"

Simbi's eyelids fluttered. Her bosom heaved and she looked down at their interlocked fingers. "But . . . you were . . . we used to be family."

Ashâke squeezed her hand. "We *are* family. Don't think you can get rid of me that easy."

Simbi burst into tears and Ashâke crushed her in a hug. "You know I didn't—" Simbi sobbed. "I never wanted—"

"Hush," said Ashâke, stroking her hair. "Hush. I know."

They remained locked in embrace, two friends, two sisters, in the middle of the dark street.

"Are you crying?" asked Simbi as she pulled back from the embrace.

"No. It's all the bloody spices. From the food. That's why I took a walk."

"Ah, spices." Simbi broke into a watery smile. And then they both began to laugh. A full-bellied laugh that rocked Ashâke's body, and stars above it was the best sound in the world. They laughed until they were clutching each other, both of them gasping for breath. And when they had spent themselves, leaning against the wall, Simbi turned to look at Ashâke and asked, a little shyly, "Would you . . . like to meet my children?"

Ashâke smiled. "I thought you'd never ask."

Epilogue

The lord of roads and crossroads followed the old path into a new world.

After Koriko had locked him away in the tree all those seasons ago he had realised the truth of their existence: that though they were orisha, that though they lorded over creation, they were bound to the very mortals who should worship them. Father had dismissed him, of course, extolling the symbiosis of such a relationship. But it troubled Eshu to think what would become of him if ever their worship ceased; it troubled him to think that he, Eshu Elegba, was held in thrall by mortals. And so he sought a way to free himself. He learned of the Fount, and found it, and drank of it.

And severed his ties with mortals.

Now, he was a god no more. He was . . . he sincerely couldn't say what he was.

He stood in a river, the murky water reaching his waist. Around him rose clumps of verdant reeds, tall stalks dancing and rustling in a slight breeze. To his left spread an endless vista of squat palm trees. In the distance three grand stone pyramids rose high into the sky, their golden points gleaming in the white sun. And beyond that, a city.

Eshu waded out of the river and onto the open road. There came the clop of hooves and the rattle of wheels, and he looked up to see a chariot approaching.

Acknowledgments

This is a tale about gods; the making and unmaking of them, and the many ways their thoughts and actions affect the lives of others. My heartfelt thanks go to the gods who surround me, whose acts in one way or the other helped guide this story from inception to completion:

Thanks to my agent, Alex Cochran, who is the god of scriveners. I couldn't have asked for a better champion. To the gods of fantastic books, my editors on both sides of the pond—Jonathan Strahan, Eli Goldman, Katie Dent, and the entire team at Tordotcom and Titan. To the god of great art, Godwin Akpan. To my siblings in godhood: Victor, for reading and taking apart an early draft of this book; Ope, for not quite managing to read those early drafts but supporting me anyway. My parents, Supreme Father and Mother, who first called me the god of stories.

And finally, to the god of completion: You, Dear Reader, who in following this story to the end have partaken in this strange alchemy of creation, ensuring that these characters live a thousand lives in your minds.

About the Author

TOBI OGUNDIRAN is the award-winning author of *Jackal, Jackal,* a collection of eighteen dark and fantastical tales, and the Guardian of the Gods duology. He has also been nominated for the British Science Fiction Association, Nommo, and Shirley Jackson Awards. His short fiction has been featured on the hit podcast *LeVar Burton Reads,* and also appears in journals such as *Lightspeed, The Magazine of Fantasy & Science Fiction, Beneath Ceaseless Skies,* and in several Year's Best anthologies. Born and raised in Nigeria, he now lives and works in the U.S. South.

tobiogundiran.com
@tobithedreamer
@tobi_thedreamer

THE BUTCHER OF THE FOREST

by Premee Mohamed

At the northern edge of a valley ruled by a ruthless foreign tyrant lies a wild forest, home to otherworldly creatures and dangerous magic. The local people know never to enter—for no one who strays into the north woods is ever seen again. No one, that is, except Veris Thorn.

When the children of the Tyrant vanish into the wood, Veris is summoned to rescue them. She has only one day before the creatures of the forest claim the children for their own. If she fails, her punishment will be swift and merciless.

To stand a chance of surviving the wood, Veris must evade traps and trickery, ancient monsters and false friends, and the haunting memory of her last journey into the forest.

Time is running short. One misstep will cost everything.

"Fast-paced, tense, fantastical and uncanny, *The Butcher of the Forest* is a perfect mix of horror and fantasy."
The New York Times

"Mohamed is one of fantasy's rising stars."
The Washington Post

WHERE THE DEAD BRIDES GATHER

by Nuzo Onoh

A powerful Nigeria-set horror tale of possession, malevolent ghosts, family tensions, secrets and murder, for readers of Octavia Butler, Ben Okri and Koji Suzuki.

Bata, a young girl tormented by nightmares, wakes up one night to find herself standing sentinel before her cousin's door. Her cousin is to get married the next morning, but only if she can escape the murderous attack of a ghost-bride, who used to be engaged to her groom.

A supernatural possession helps Bata battle and vanquish the vengeful ghost bride, and following a botched exorcism, she is transported to Ibaja-La, the realm of dead brides. There, she receives secret powers to fight malevolent ghost-brides before being sent back to the human realm, where she must learn to harness her new abilities as she strives to protect those whom she loves.

By turns touching and terrifying, this is vivid supernatural horror story of family drama, long-held secrets, possession, death - and what lies beyond.

"Nuzo Onoh is a wordsmith who has earned the moniker The Queen of African Horror.."
Tananarive Due, author of *The Reformatory*

TITANBOOKS.COM

THE NAMING SONG

by Jedediah Berry

When something fell from the something tree, all the words went away. And the world changed.

Monsters slipped from dreams. The land began to shift, and ghosts wandered the world in trances. Only with the rise of the named and their committees—Maps, Ghosts, Dreams, and Names—could humanity stand against the terrors of the nameless wilds. Now, they build borders, shackle ghosts and hunt monsters. The nameless are to be fought, and feared.

One unnamed courier of the names committee travels aboard the Number Twelve train, assigning names to the people and things that need them. Her position on the train grants her safety in a world that otherwise fears her. But when she accidentally pulls a monster from a dream, and attacks by the nameless rock the Number Twelve, she is forced to flee. Accompanied by a patchwork ghost, a fretful monster, and a nameless animal who prowls the borders between realities, she sets out to look for her long-lost sister.

Her search for the truth of her own life opens the door to a revolutionary future—for the words she carries will reshape the world.

"A brilliant, thrilling adventure"
Holly Black, *New York* Times bestselling author

For more fantastic fiction, author events,
exclusive excerpts, competitions, limited editions and more

VISIT OUR WEBSITE
titanbooks.com

LIKE US ON FACEBOOK
facebook.com/titanbooks

FOLLOW US ON TWITTER AND INSTAGRAM
@TitanBooks

EMAIL US
readerfeedback@titanemail.com